In This Earth and In Heaven

In This Earth and In Heaven

Kennith Swinford

SANTA FE

Sunstone books may be purchased for educational, business, or sales promotional use. For information please write: Special Markets Department, Sunstone Press, P.O. Box 2321, Santa Fe, New Mexico 87504-2321.

Book and Cover design ≈ Vicki Ahl
Body typeface ≈ Univers
Printed on acid free paper

Library of Congress Cataloging-in-Publication Data

Swinford, Kennith, 1934-
   In this earth and in heaven / by Kennith Swinford.
      p. cm.
   ISBN 978-0-86534-766-3 (pbk. : alk. paper)
   1. Indians--Mixed descent--Fiction. 2. Inheritance and succession--Fiction.
   3. Coal mines and mining--New Mexico--Fiction. I. Title.
   PS3619.W55I5 2010
   813'.6--dc22

                              2010016237

Published in

WWW.SUNSTONEPRESS.COM
SUNSTONE PRESS / POST OFFICE BOX 2321 / SANTA FE, NM 87504-2321 /USA
(505) 988-4418 / ORDERS ONLY (800) 243-5644 / FAX (505) 988-1025

*P*ROLOGUE

At first there were only sheepmen. Then came the
Cattlemen. Just a few of them. But those few came with their
Cattle and horses, vaqueros and Chryslers and,
Most important of all, their money.

They came during the depression. Young men mostly.
Breaking away from rich family-owned ranches in Texas and
Oklahoma to start their own dynasty on the great plains of
New Mexico. And with their abundance of family money,
They bought the sheepmen's land,
Who then shifted westward. But after the cattlemen
Had bought the land, built their massive ranch
Houses, shipped in their cattle, and moved their cowboys into
Bunkhouses and the sheepmen's shanties, they found one
Sheepman remained. One man, Beauford Gavolin,
Had refused the cattle baron's
Money and
Continued raising sheep on some of the finest
And some of the poorest land in New Mexico.

"Just one...one dirty lousy stinking sheepherder left,"
Les Smith, the county's largest cattleman and a neighbor
Had complained. He couldn't beg, buy or gamble
For the land that belonged to the old hard shell,
Bible totin' sonofabitch.
He guessed he would wait
For the old one armed bastard to die
And then buy from his daughter.
And if she wouldn't sell,
He would sure as hell steal that piece of land,
From her house to the Flying S. They didn't use it anyway.
No good for sheep. No water and too many rattlesnakes.

Beauford Gavolin died of old age, and not
A broken heart.
People who attended his sermons,
And funeral, surmised that
His precious daughter, Ruby,
Had precipitated a premature death. She had given birth
To an out-of-wedlock son. A half-breed. He hated the sin but loved
The little sucker as well as his daughter. He died
A happy man, with his only burden being fear
That he might have killed a Mexican that Les Smith
Had hired to scare him off his own land.

But even after the old sheepman's death, the rancher
Couldn't buy the land. He lied, "I'm offering you three times
What yore land is worth." She refused to sell. "This land
Is for my son," she argued. He was her pride, her
Hope, her life. "Maybe someday he will buy
The Flying S from you and raise
Sheep on it." "That's a bunch
Of b.s.," he couldn't resist. He paused and stared
At her. "You are one crazy bitch." Without another word
He stormed toward his pickup.

Ruby Gavolin hired a man to do the work
Of her father and continued to raise, shear and sell sheep.
And the land
Between her house and the Flying S, that Les Smith
So desperately desired, lay blistering beneath the New Mexico Sun.
And the years passed. Eight, ten, twelve. Eddy was seventeen.
And it was almost daylight. And a voice rang out, "Whore."

1

When the dawn began to break, its lightness revealed the outline of the sheep-woman's small frame house silhouetted against the sparsely vegetated hill country of Southeastern New Mexico. The yellowish glow of a single bulb spilled through a kitchen window and splattered upon the parched ground outside. The smell of frying bacon filtered through the cracked board siding of the wind battered structure, mixing into the crisp morning air. The noses of the trained sheep dogs twitched at the aroma as they pulled themselves up, stretched and shook. Then they jumped off the front porch, loped around the back of the house to await their scraps of gravy, meat and biscuit. The wind whistled off the butte out behind the house, and the old windmill began to sluggishly revolve. The screeching of the pump stirred the sheep, which had been huddled together for protection against marauding coyotes. The ewes began to bleat to their young, urging relief of swollen udders.

The sun was about to break over the horizon, as the drunken voice bellowed from the kitchen once again. "Gaddamn whore." The man's face was red and swollen. His breath reeked of the smell of alcohol. His eyes were bloodshot and bleary. "Nothing but a low down, belly lickin, Indian-lovin, slut whore."

The woman when younger might have been pretty. Not now. Her face and body showed the years of sun and wind, work and hardships. Her hair hung straight and graying across strong shoulders and small sagging breasts. Ruby Gavolin turned from the stove and spoke wearily, "Hush up Lester. You're drunk. You say crazy things when you been out all night drinkin and dickerin around."

"I recon I been drinkin and dickerin," he snapped at her. "I got rights same as you. Sides, it's your fault, not mine. Just been tryin to cleanse my soul of yore sins." He banged the bottle he had been nursing against the kitchen table top. "What man who had an Indian lover fer a bed partner wouldn't drink and dicker? Huh?" He screamed, "Who wouldn't?"

The woman pushed a steaming cup of coffee in front of him, while wondering if it wasn't about time for her to run his sorry ass off. He had provided her with companionship and some work. And she had desperately needed him after her daddy had died, but things were not the same now. She had become frightened of him because of his heavy drinking. When he sobered, they would talk.

Lester Snodgrass slammed his hand against the cup, knocking it half way across the kitchen. "Whore coffee."

"Behave yourself Lester, you'll wake the boy."

"Who gives a good damn if I wake the boy?" He unscrewed the lid from the bottle, moved it to his lips and emptied it. "His Daddy maybe?" He hurled the bottle across the room, not blinking, when it crashed against the wall. "Yeah, maybe his dark skinned daddy might give a damn about em."

The woman stood tense, suspicious of a serious confrontation. She pleaded, "Please Lester, don't talk like that. You're drunk."

You made me a drunk when you squirted out that Indian squealer, and I didn't even know you then."

"You right about that Lester. My son was here before you and you sure didn't have to come here if you didn't want to."

He banged his fist against the table. "I bet I know his daddy. Bet it was the Indian bastard that was over here yesterday. You thought I didn't see him. You thought I was in the high pasture with the sheep. I saw him. Rode right up here to the house."

She interrupted, "He was just looking for some of the Flying S strays Lester. That's all."

"Bullcrap," he snarled. "Lookin fer strays you say. I'd say he was looking fer a stray piece. That's whut I'd say. He was looking fer a stray piece." He moved toward her, and pushed his finger close to her face." And if I'd been in town, you would have give it to em, wouldn't ya?" He made a fist and shook it. "Huh? You'd let him had it."

She had no intention of answering such a stupid question. Her affair with Dan Silvercloud had been over seventeen years.

He slapped her in the face and hollered, "Wouldn't you have give it to him?"

Ruby Gavolin jumped back. Her face, red with anger. Scared but determined, she picked up one of the table chairs. "Don't ever touch me again Lester Snodgrass."

His mouth dropped open. Saliva ran from the corners. He wiped his whiskered chin with the back of his hand. He pounded the table with his fist, and yelled at the top of his lungs, "Indian lovin whore."

Seventeen year old Eddy Gavolin lay motionless in the early dusk of his small upstairs bedroom. Staring at nothing, his heart pounding. Slowly piecing together his past. The darkness of his skin, and hair. Lester's resentment toward him. His mother's overbearing protection. The drinking. The fighting. Why?

In the kitchen, Lester was clumsily searching through the cupboard. He found another bottle, almost empty. He popped the cork, swallowed a mouthful and glared. "I'm gonna kill you Ruby, fer whut you done to me. Told everbody in town we wuz married. That I had adopted the little Indian bastard. I ain't married nobody, and I ain't adopted no kid."

She sat the chair down. "We common-law, Lester. Same as."

"Made a fool outta me Ruby. Screwin the Indian right under my nose. Now you gonna pay." He sucked the last swallow from the bottle and took a step toward her. "You are a dead woman Ruby. I'm gonna kill your sorry butt."

She screamed.

Eddy pushed the cover back, jumped out of bed, and scampered across the room. He had often heard them fussin and cussin, but never heard her scream. Nervously he wrapped his sweating hands around his granddaddy's loaded carbine hanging on the wall. As he opened the door he heard his mother begging, "Don't do nothing stupid Lester."

"I'm gonna kill you Ruby, fer screwin that Indian."

Eddy Gavolin slithered down the stairs and rushed to the kitchen. He stepped into the room and leveled the barrel of the gun before speaking. "You ain't gonna kill nobody Pop."

"Hear that Ruby? He still calls me Pop." The drunk whirled around and stared for a minute at the carbine. "You think you bad with that gun boy. Bad like yore old grandpappy was?"

"Bet he never backed down from nobody. Ain't that right Momma?"

"You don't know nothing boy. Don't even know where you come from. You sure didn't come from my blood. You is a half-breed."

Ruby lunged toward him gritting her teeth and swinging her clinched fist.

Eddy pulled her back. "Let him speak his peace Momma. I recon I'm old enough to know where I come from." He released her arm and stepped between them.

Lester stepped backward, jerked open a cabinet drawer and groped for the handle of a butcher knife. He turned pointing the long blade toward Ruby. "You come from that slut there. That's where you come from."

She pushed her back against the wall. Her face, strained and sweating. Tears were forming and her eyes were burning.

"You ain't no blood of mine boy." Lester advanced toward her with the knife. "You got Indian blood in you."

Eddy had known that since grade school. The other kids never missed an opportunity to remind him.

"Look at them tears boy." Lester laughed. " She ought to thought bout that fore she let that Injun to her. Ain't that right boy?"

The youth's body jerked. "Shut up." He started to say Pop, but thought. "Shut up, you hear. You ain't been no daddy to me. You treated me worse than the sheep dogs ever since you been here."

"My soul is clean boy." Lester was capable of making himself believe something whether it was right or wrong. He pointed the knife at Ruby. "That whore there, will be going to Hell today for what she done."

"Maybe she had a reason," Eddy interjected. He shifted the carbine. "And as long as I got this gun, only one likely to be going to Hell today, is you. You better leave right now and head on down that road."

The drunk tightened his grip on the knife. "Bastard kids don't boss me round."

Eddy was furious. "You better get your butt off this property fore I shoot it off."

"Don't smartass me boy. I made you decent. I gave you my name."

"You might have given it to me, but I wouldn't have it. I'm Eddy Gavolin. Not Eddy Snodgrass."

Lester pointed the knife at Eddy and moved toward him. "You who I want you to be."

Ruby stepped between them and screamed, "Don't go near that boy Lester."

He jerked the knife up and lunged toward her.

Grandpappy's old carbine was cocked and ready. Eddy squeezed the trigger, felt the impact, and saw red appear through Lester's shirt. The concussion rattled the windows.

The big man did not fall. He pressed his free hand against the wound in his stomach. With his teeth gritted, and the knife still raised, with one quick movement he plunged it into her chest.

"Bitch," he mumbled, as both went to the floor.

Then silence.

The bright morning sun flooded through the kitchen windows now. Ruby Gavolin's eyes flickered. Her lips moved. "Son."

Eddy had been paralyzed, too frightened to move. Her weak voice moved him to reality. He dropped the gun and began to tremble as he moved to her. He fell to his knees beside her and pushed Lester off her. The drunk looked up at him. His voice gurgled. "You little bastard. You gut shot me."

"Son," her voice now weaker.

Eddy moved closer. "I'll get you a doctor, Momma."

"Wait." Her mind was blurry but the one thing he must know. "I love you Son."

"I know Momma."

Her eyes were closed now. A faint smile on her face. "I've got somebody to pass the land down to. My prayers were answered." She gently squeezed his hand, "I'm so proud of you Eddy."

He thought she was going to tell him who his real dad was. Her last words were barely audible, "Don't ever let Les Smith build a fence across our land."

"Don't worry Momma." He gently kissed her forehead. "Everything is going to be okay."

The smile on her face faded.

"Ruby, your little bastard gut shot me."

She didn't hear those words.

2

*R*uby Gavolin Snodgrass was declared dead upon her arrival at the San Sonora, New Mexico Hospital. Lester was expected to live and stand trial for her death.

Her funeral was held on the following Saturday. It was a brisk, cold day. Dark black clouds hung in the sky, moving southerly, as cold north wind spilled across the small desert cemetery.

An old Indian woman tightened her hand-woven shawl around her shoulders as sleet peppered down. Her daughter-in-law pulled her dark skinned daughter Sonya nearer to the warmth of her hefty body. Both were dressed in gaily colored dresses. Her son Damond, dressed in faded denim jeans and leather fringed coat, stood at her side. Both Sonya and Damond had ridden the bus to school with Eddy. Actually her son Damond had been the only classmate of Eddy Gavolin attending the funeral. Behind them, wearing the typical western duster, his sweat stained Stetson held tightly against his chest, stood the father of the children.

Big Dan Silvercloud, as his uncle before him, was now the Indian foreman of the vast Flying S Ranch. His leathery face strained, hiding emotional memories of the past. A decorated Vietnam hero, and a proud man. Proud of his children, proud of his expectant wife, and proud of his position on the ranch. But he was a burdened man. Burdened with guilt. A guilt clear and distinct. A guilt he hoped would be buried forever with the internment of the sheep woman's body. However he knew that it would not be forgotten. It would revisit his mind and soul each time he remembered her, or looked upon the mixed blood youth sitting graveside.

Among the others attending was Jake Wilson, president of San Sonora State Bank. In the old days Beauford Gavolin had been one of the bank's premier customers. Owner of one of the largest sheep ranches in the area, he could well remember when he had been quite successful. But that was before his feud with Les Smith over the few sections of 'no man's land' between his house and the Flying S. In that squabble he had also lost the use of his left arm which had contributed to his slow-down. Since then he had been content, with Ruby's help, to earn a modest living on the ranch. However this situation had created an opportunity for him to spend more time to serve as a fire and brimstone hard-shell Baptist preacher. He had made many a mile in that old pickup truck, sometime on horseback, to serve the needs of small country churches in that area. And often, the meager love offerings were returned to families in need, before his departure. Jake Wilson respected a man of his genteel quality and felt it a justified honor in attending his daughter's funeral.

Deputy Sheriff Dave Brinkle was there with his wife, sitting next to Eddy. The deputy had his arm around the youth. After his mother's death they had invited him to stay with them, since no known family members could be located. In that short few days before the funeral, Dave and Mrs. Brinkle had developed a strange closeness to the youth. The county judge sensed this, and mentioned the possibility of appointing Dave Brinkle as Eddy's guardian.

Lambert Snodgrass, Lester's brother was sitting to the left of Eddy, their shoulders touching. Years before, they had arrived from the Piney woods of East Texas to seek employment in the oil fields of Eastern New Mexico. They stopped in San Sonora. Lambert was hired the next day by Drake Oil Company. Lester had not been so fortunate. Because of his drinking he had to settle for a low paying job as a short order cook. Later he was demoted to dishwasher. A couple years later he met Ruby at a rundown dance hall outside San Sonora. Ironically the same place she had met the tall, flashy, Marine, Dan Silvercloud several years before.

They had all come to show their respect.

Les Smith was standing at the graveside, maybe not so much to show his respect, but to approach Eddy afterwards in regard to the sale of the sheep ranch. He wanted to get this taken care of before the youth could move away.

The thin frail undertaker was now shivering. It was getting colder.

"Amen."

Eddy rose and shook the preacher's hand.

"Bless you my son." He shook a few more hands, then hurried off toward his car. The wind flopping his coat tail. His tie fluttering over his shoulder.

Eddy stepped to the edge of the cavity in the earth beneath the casket and dropped something in. He did not cry. Near the bottom the earth was a dark gray silt. Coal. He never envisioned the impact the black stuff would someday have upon his young life. He just wished he had a load of sand from White Sands to cover her with. He would do that someday. She deserved that. He looked at the wreaths. Counted five. He then turned and lit out toward Lambert's new Pontiac. Lambert had wanted to talk to him about something before returning to the rig.

Les Smith had been watching Eddy. He intercepted him before he could reach the car and was puffing when he took Eddy's hand and spoke, "Sure sorry to hear about your folks, Son."

Eddy quickly released the old man's hand and waited. He wasn't really interested in what he had to say but figured he might as well get it over with.

The rancher stared at the ground. "Probably ain't a real good time to talk about business." He looked at Eddy. "Seein you might be needin some pocket money." He paused. "School'n'all." He sucked in a lungful of cold air. "Wanted to talk to you about buyin yore mama's property. Recon you're the rightful owner now."

The old coot couldn't even wait till the dirt was over his mother. Eddy turned toward the car. "You wastin your time Mister Smith."

"Hold on now Son." He half-way blocked his path. "Least think about it." He could sense Eddy's aggravation and for sure wanted to get the offer in before he walked off. "No hard feelings ye hear. I'll give you fifty thousand fer that old wore out sheep ranch. And you can sell the animals. That's a lot of money for that old pore desert land and that old bare butte out back of the house. Onliest thing worth much out ther is the timber and that little mountain stream that runs across over at the back."

"Forget it Mister Smith." As he pushed by the old man, Eddy remarked, "Buy your land someday, maybe."

A chill crept up Les Smith's spine, but not from the cold. Dammit, he thought. He was kicking up sand all the way back to his black Chrysler. To hell with the three hundred dollar handmade boots.

Eddy scooted into the car and before shutting the door hollered, "Don't want to see any of your fence crews on Gavolin land between our house and your house Mister Smith. I'll shoot their asses off."

His Mother had warned him his grandpappy had lost the use of his arm while feuding with the rancher's attempts to build a fence across their property.

3

*E*lection time had come and gone in San Sonora. Deputy Brinkle was now sheriff. He had accepted Eddy's guardianship and moved him into a small garage apartment behind their home. There, he and his wife could keep a watchful eye on him making sure he ate and dressed properly. Also make sure he attended school regularly. The court had granted the sale of the horses, saddles, dogs and sheep on the ranch. The money could be used for the youth's well-being and education. And as guardian, Sheriff Brinkle would be in control of the distribution.

Eddy would be a senior when the summer vacation ended and school resumed. He had missed his mom terribly, but found that living in town was great fun. He had often regretted having sold his horse and saddle, but realized trying to keep them was not feasible. Someday, when he settled down he would buy another bigger and finer animal. He also wished he still had those two old prize winning sheep. Now he didn't have a blessed thing to show at the F.F.A. shows. He sure would miss that, because often on those trips out of town, the truck would be so crowded that Betty Branigan would sit in his lap. That had felt real good and he sure would miss that. Then them old lazy sheep dogs. He sure did miss them rascals.

His spirits sure had been lifted when "Coach" told him he had made the football team. One of the assistant coaches had spotted him playing soccer with some of the Hispanic and Indian boys down at the Catholic church. He told the head coach, "That kid can nearly kick the bladder out of it." They invited him to the football field for a workout, and no doubt he would be their punter. But the team needed a field goal kicker also. They lined him up in front of the goal post. He kicked straight on and he missed it a mile. He really felt uncomfortable kicking, straight on, but tried several more misses. While the coach and the assistant were discussing other alternatives for a field goal kicker, Eddy sat the ball on the tee. He leaned it a bit, eyed the goalpost and backed off at an angle. To him that felt more comfortable. He approached the ball, hit it soccer style, and it split the uprights at forty yards.

"Hot damn," the coach remarked. "Did you see that?"

End of discussion.

The band was working out on the other end of the field. Eddy stopped by to watch. Coach had given him a tee and ball and invited him to come by the practice field any time to work out. And that football under his arm sure made him feel important. Boy that head majorette sure was pretty.

School had started now and Eddy had made the team as their kicker. And now, unknown to her, he had developed a deep secret love for Gloria Drake. She was the richest, prettiest, and most popular girl in school, but Eddy wasn't privy to that fact. And since the kicker didn't spend a lot of time on the field, he didn't miss a chance to check her out on the sideline. Her skimpy uniform sure did turn him on and he loved her dearly, even though he realized she had the hots for Jimmy Muhler. Of course, Jimmy was their all-district quarterback, and the richest boy in school. A matched pair, one could say.

Eddy's senior year bordered on phenomenal. The season was going well, not because of his kicking ability, but the excellent quarterbacking of Jimmy Muhler. And his most memorable moment was, not when he had kicked a game winning field-goal in the last second, but when Gloria Drake ran out on the field and hugged him. He was proud to wear the uniform but his shoulder pads and helmet had restricted some of the pleasure. He could smell her perfume. Boy, he sure wouldn't forget that moment. And at least she knew he existed.

Seemingly, Eddy was being accepted by the in crowd. Probably not because of his association with Sheriff Brinkle, or because of his kicking ability, but because of his deserted sheep ranch. It had become a play Mecca for the school's elite.

During football season, Mr. Green, the honors science teacher had asked permission from Sheriff Brinkle and Eddy to haul his class to the ranch for climbing classes. This field trip, he proposed to the principal, would be a great learning opportunity for the class. Eddy was not smart enough to be in the class but Gloria Drake was. He begged the sheriff for the permit with conditions that he could be excused from school to go along to keep an eye on everything. Gloria mostly.

Mr. Green had parked the bus in front of a place at the face of the butte, not terribly precarious. A good place for beginners to learn. They unloaded their rented gear and the teaching experience began. Safety first. Mr.Green was an experienced climber and the talented students learned quickly about the safety equipment.

The climb began. Eddy was the first to the top with a rope. He secured it and the others started up. Gloria had been a little scared and the safety gear had felt comforting, especially on the way down. At noon they traveled to the Dairy Bar for hamburgers and a bathroom break. That afternoon they would return for a lesson on repelling. Eddy knew nothing about that, but was eager to learn.

The students had nick-named the butte, Nasty Butt.

After football season, and after the first good snow had fallen, Eddy had invited Gloria and some of her friends back to the ranch for skiing down the backside of the butte. That's where he had learned the art. His mother could ski and some of his most memorable moments were when they would throw their skis in the back of the pickup and head for the mountains. The mountains were much more of a challenge. Actually, he considered himself a decent skier and assumed he would be better than any of the other students there. Wrong! He was probably not as good as

Gloria. He had not been aware that her father owned a ski resort near Ruidoso.

It was a clear cold sunshiny day. Their feet made crunching noises in the snow as they trekked up the back side of old Nasty Butt. When they reached the top, they strapped on their skies. A lot of laughing going on as who would be the first one down. One person remarked that she probably would have to go down on her rear-end if she got down. Jimmy made the remark that if he had his hang glider he would sail down. Gloria showed out a bit, and then started helping Jimmy. Eddy showed out a bit more, and started helping the girl that couldn't ski. The other pair could ski a little and moved down the hill. Half-way down, Jimmy had reached a point where he could slowly move, without falling. The girl Eddy was helping was learning faster.

Gloria felt competitive. She looked over at Eddy and smiled, "I'll race you to the bottom."

He pulled the brim of his western hat snuggly around his forehead and pointed to a steeper part of the slope. "Take off."

She was good. He struggled to catch her and finally did. She slowed a bit and let him pass.

Just before hitting the end of the slope she hollered, "Gotcha." Then she deliberately ran over him.

They hit the snow holding each other and laughing. She was lying on top of him. He thought he could feel her taunt breasts beneath their heavy clothing. Perhaps he was only fantasizing. He was so hot he was sure his backside was melting the snow.

"I beat you," she said as she rolled off him

"Nope," he replied as he jumped to his feet. With strong shoulders and arms, he reached down and gently helped her to her feet.

She smiled. "Thanks," and began brushing snow.

Eddy was so enthralled he didn't realize he had lost his hat. She reminded him. He retrieved it and shook off the snow. They gathered their skis and walked over to await the others who were still moving slowly down the slope.

Gloria hoped Jimmy wouldn't be peed off at her. He was.

In the spring Mr. Green envisioned another field trip for his honors class to old Nasty Butt. This time, Jimmy Muhler had agreed to bring his hang glider out for a presentation on aerodynamics. Owning such an unusual contraption was not a problem for him. His dad owned Muhler Aviation Company in San Sonora. He manufactured a single engine airplane and the company had become very successful. Jimmy had been piloting since sixteen.

Jimmy and Eddy hauled the knocked down glider to the ranch in a trailer pulled behind Eddy's pickup. The bus followed. Jimmy smoked a joint on the way. That surprised Eddy. He would have to fumigate the truck.

After they arrived, they unloaded and Jimmy explained the simplicity of putting the glider together. Mr. Green then taught a short aeronautical lesson on sailing without power. They picked it up and headed up the hill. All but two. One of the students said she had a side ache. Mr. Green volunteered to stay with her. Eddy suggested she lie down in the front seat of his pickup and stretch out.

Excitedly, they tromped up the hill, laughing and talking. One of the boys remarked, "Hope Jim don't bust his butt on old Nasty Butt."

Gloria stuck close to Jimmy's side.

When they reached a suitable altitude, and the wind condition seemed right, Jimmy halted the group. They turned the glider and he made preparation for the flight. "Dammit." He had left snaps for the harness in Eddy's pickup. Eddy volunteered to retrieve them.

Eddy jogged down the hill to the truck. He could hear the radio blaring. The passenger door was open. A towel was hanging over the window of the closed driver's side door. Eddy assumed, to keep the sun out. He jerked the door open. Her stomach must have witnessed a miraculous recovery. The student's pants were off. The teacher's pants were down. Eddy grabbed the snaps off the dash, promised to never tell, and slammed the door shut.

On the way back up Eddy pondered why the hankering for

sex had been denied him. The female students seemed warm and friendly, but had not responded to his manly desires. He wondered if his past, or the darkness of his skin, might be offensive to them. He wondered if Gloria and Jimmy might be getting it on. He loved her so much. He was glad school was almost out. He wanted to leave San Sonora. He would call Lambert about that roughnecking job. He was plenty ready to make him some of that big oil-field money.

4

New Mexico, land of enchantment. Land of prosperity and poverty. Land of nature's bountiful beauty. Land of excitement. A land where people of different ethnic backgrounds bonded in peace and lived fruitful lives. A land divided East and West by the beautiful Rio Grande. A land that can be traveled endlessly with one's vision drinking in the grandeur of majestic snow capped mountains, fertile valleys, bountiful green forests, colorful deserts, mammoth canyons, sun drenched mesas, and sparkling white sands. Beautiful sites, bountiful in the state. There is Carlsbad Caverns, ancient Indian Pueblos, abandoned forts, Spanish Missions, and exotic plazas touting beautiful artwork, wood carvings and handmade Turquoise jewelry.

A land of wealth. Active oil and gas fields, abundant timber expanses, vast uranium production, and bountiful farms and ranches.

A land where tavern lights burn till late in the night. Where blood and passion run hot after a day in the fields, or at a sawmill, or on a shift in the oil fields, or on a military base. Where sometime the bartender would have to assist the remaining few toward the door at closing time. Earlier there had sat a lonesome girl looking for companionship, a home sick Private, a disgruntled worker from the atomic laboratory, an off duty Ranger, a drunk Mexican, a cowboy flirting with a brooding wife, an Indian asleep at a corner table, and a hippy stoned on LSD trying to keep his distance from a rough looking drilling crew.

Lambert Snodgrass had bought another new Pontiac and compared to Eddy's old farm pickup it seemed to float down the desert road. They had traveled eastward for endless miles since leaving San Sonora. And they had not seen much of anything but a few cows, a few windmills, a gas station and a motel. However they had seen a lot of sand and mesquite. To Eddy it seemed as if they must be damned near to Texas.

They both were doing some serious thinking.

Lambert Snodgrass was Lester's younger brother all right, and had realized he was plenty sorry. He just hadn't thought he would do something so stupid as to kill a woman. She had been taking care of him for years. He did know, however, that he had a mean streak in him and drank too much. Not that he was some kind of saint, he still knew he was a better man than Lester. He reckoned that state prison might be taking some of that mean streak out of him. One thing for sure, he had felt sorry for Eddy and had been sending him a little spending money. Even though he knew Eddy was worth more than he was, he had offered him a job after the funeral.

Eddy was reliving memories of his past. His loving mother, who had accepted disgrace in order to fulfill her desire for passion or pregnancy. He had not known which. Her decision, after his grandpappy's death, to live unmarried, with another man. His true father, unknown to him, who had accepted a moment of passion even with the risk of impregnation of his Indian blood. Sheriff Dave Brinkle, his guardian and godfather who had comforted him in time of need, guided him, befriended him. His prominent fellow classmates who, he suspected, used him and the ranch for their personal pleasure, then discriminated against him at their lavish parties. What the hell? He was gone now from San Sonora. When he returned he hoped things would be different. "I will show the sonofabitches," he mumbled while visualizing the delicate white skin of some of his classmate's stomachs against that of his own.

"What did you say?" Lambert asked, turning down the radio.

"Aw nothing," Eddy replied. "Just thinking."

"About what?" He looked over and smiled. "Poontang."

Eddy smiled for the first time since leaving San Sonora. "How did you know?"

"Cause that's what I was thinking about." He looked at Eddy. "Better than thinking bout work, ain't it."

"Yep!"

"Better get some good thinking in now. Won't have time to think about it when we hit that rig floor." He turned the radio back up. "What kind of music you like, Eddy?"

"Everbody at school likes rock."

"If you gonna hang with me, better like country. Don't like that long hair crap." He looked over at Eddy. "You're a man now."

That sure made Eddy feel good.

"Speaking of hair, you bout ready for one? If it gets too long, I might screw it in between two drill stem." He smiled. "I screw purty fast. That is, when I get them big diesels purring."

Eddy's hair was not much longer than his classmates. He liked it but would get it cut shorter because he sure was ready to be a man now. He wanted to be a real man just like Lambert. He remembered when Lambert would occasionally visit the sheep ranch to visit Lester. He was a sharp dresser and always drove a fine automobile, sometimes a convertible. Often he would be with a young woman. He had impressed him since he had reached adolescence and Eddy had accessed him of being a real cocksman.

Eddy liked the idea of dressing in a good hat, fancy belt buckle, and handmade boots. He also would like moving around to different places in a fine car, and chasing women everywhere he went. He was tired of being called a Kid, Boy, Injun, and most of all Bastard. Anybody tried that again, he would for sure clean their plow, or they would have to clean his.

They were entering a small town.

"Want a hamburger?" Lambert asked.

"Why not?" Lambert buzzed by the first little café without stopping. Eddy figured they didn't serve beer there or there was not a pretty waitress on duty.

They stopped at the next one and Lambert did know the waitress.

She winked at Eddy. "You are twenty-one ain't you Big Boy?"

Eddy nodded.

While wolfing down the beer and burger, Eddy asked again. "How much did you say I'd be making?" It was the same amount as quoted before and a hell-of-a-lot more than working at that gas station that Sheriff Brinkle had suggested. However it would be seven days a week.

"Course there will be times when the rig is moved to another drill site. When that happens the crew's got rec time." He grinned, "Or tail time."

Eddy would like that.

Lambert laid a generous tip on the table.

The waitress rushed over. "Good to see you Lambert." She eased against Eddy and pinched him on the butt. "Come to see me sometime, Sweety."

He sure was going to like this oil field work.

She removed the bill from the table, and pushed it into her bra. They were big and Eddy could tell there was plenty more room in that big cavity.

She gathered up the baskets and beer cans. "Ya'll come back now, ye hear."

They were back on the road now. It was the hottest part of the day and the air conditioner was going full blast till it had cooled the interior off. Eddy turned it down a notch or two. "Sure appreciate you giving me this job Lambert."

"I like single men like you on my crew. Most married men can't stay with it. Too much movin around." Lambert glanced over at Eddy. "They get used to sleeping under a gown tail ever nite and have a hard time staying away from it."

Eddy laughed again. "What you got against gown tails Lambert?"

"Nothing against the tail. Just the gown. Don't need to get too attached to them just yet. Someday maybe."

Eddy had not been offended at Lambert calling him Kid.

"I'll show you what I mean when we get settled in. We'll get us some."

Eddy got all excited. He assumed his virginal existence would soon be coming to an end. "How much further Bert?"

"To the plant, to the rig, or to the tang?"

"The plant."

"Bout twenty minutes."

"How long you been working for Drake Oil, Lambert?"

"Nearly twenty years."

Eddy considered it odd that he was about to go to work for Thomas Drake. The man who had fathered the girl of his dreams. God how he loved her. He loved her so much he could just eat her. But then there was Jimmy Muhler. The sonofabitch had got a football scholarship to Texas Tech and wanted her to go there too. Eddy couldn't figure out why he couldn't have got a scholarship to Notre Dame. After all, his family was Catholic. Course, Jimmy didn't have much religion at all, that he knew of.

"Can't believe it's been damn near twenty years." He paused and remembered. "Me and Lester came out here with him from Houston. He was a young crazy wildcatter and I was a younger crazier roughneck. Lester was older."

Eddy interrupted. "Was Lester a roughneck?"

"Naw. He was a cook, and a damn good one. Thomas had told him, when he hit it big, he was going to build a hotel with a fine steakhouse in it. He would want him to cook." Lambert shook his head. "And sure as hell, he did hit it big when he brought in that little ole field up north of San Sonora. And he did build him a hotel with a steak-house in it."

Eddy remembered the hotel well. The only five story building in town. On the interior, an atrium ran to the top. As a youngster he could remember entering the huge front door with his mother. As they walked past the desk he gazed upward and forward simultaneously. His young mind was bewildered. He just couldn't believe his own eyes. She squeezed his hand tightly. Across the lobby a glass enclosed elevator traversed the distance to fourth floor. It traveled with exposed cables inside a simulated oil derrick. Probably an idea only a wildcatter could have envisioned. At the fourth floor, you exited the main elevator. A private one carried you to the penthouse.

Eddy was so excited he about peed in his pants. He was going to get to ride that thing all the way to the top.

She dragged him to the desk.

The balding desk clerk turned toward her. "May I help you?"

"I brought my son up here to ride your elevator."

He looked over his glasses. "Do you have a room here?"

"Nope we just come to ride the elevator. I'll pay you for the ride."

The clerk was annoyed that she had brought her little Papoose to a fine establishment like the Drake for an elevator ride. Why not let the little Pooper shimmy up the flag pole out on the street and slide down. That's what most of the other kids that came to town did. "I'm sorry Madam, that would be against the rules. You must have a room here to ride our elevator."

She had been plenty pissed off. She didn't want a room, she just wanted a ride. If her daddy had been here things would have been different. More especially if he had been packing his forty-five in that shoulder holster beneath that old black coat. Beauford would have quoted him a verse or two from the Bible, pulled his coat back deliberately to where the clerk could see the sidearm. Then he would have said, "The boy wants to ride." But her daddy was gone, and didn't seem much she could do. She dragged her son toward the door.

Eddy could well remember, he cried all the way to the truck. Now he was going to work for the Son-of-a-bitch who built the place. On top of that he was in love with his daughter. Eddy's mind switched over to Gloria. He remembered her in those boots and tights. He remembered the trip to the ranch to ski. He could relate to every moment that transpired in any day.

Lambert's voice broke his concentration. "I can remember when Thomas didn't have a pot to pee in." He laughed. "Or a window to throw it out. When he left Houston after his divorce from his first wife, all he had left was one old wore out rig, the clothes on his back and his credit. Lucky bastard didn't stay down long." Lambert eased the car around a Greyhound bus. "Moved that old piece of junk out here, beat some Indians and ranchers out of their leases, and hit big on the first hole. Everything he's touched since has turned to gold." He looked over at Eddy. "You bout to go to sleep?"

Eddy shook his head. "What you reckon he's worth?"

"Millions. He's a con man. A fast talker. Can talk a man outta his lease or a woman outta her drawers. His money spends as good as anybody's and he's damn good to work for."

A few more miles passed. In silence. "How much Indian blood you think I got in me Lambert?"

"Don't look like you're half. But what to hell? Lots of people got Indian blood in em, and damn proud of it." Lambert slowed the vehicle and pointed. "Well Kid, there she is."

It was a desert oasis with its tall gleaming water tower. And being the majority stockholder gave Thomas Drake the authority to paint his Drake insignia on the side of it. Near the tower, neat rows of white frame company houses were sitting on inviting lush green lawns. And in the background was the refinery. Its smokestacks, separators, motors, storage tanks, flares and its unpleasant odors. Surrounding this monstrosity were the gas wells, their Christmas trees releasing a steady flow of raw gas into this contraption which devours, digests and then pushes the treated gas into a network of pipelines.

"Really something ain't it?" Lambert asked.

"Smells like Mother Nature cut loose with the big one, don't it?"

"Better get used to it. You're not on a sheep ranch now. You're in the oil patch now and the gas stinks worse than manure."

Eddy pointed over to the houses. "We gonna live in one of them?"

Naw. Them's for the people working out here. We'll be living in a motel in town."

Eddy liked that idea. Probably wouldn't be any young single girls living way out here anyway.

Lambert stopped the car in front of the office and looked

over toward the white crushed rock runway. "Damn old Thomas done beat us here, but we ain't late."

Eddy looked over at the twin prop. Sleek and beautiful. A green Drake with a yellow bill painted on its side. Damn he would like to be rich. Then he could buy whatever he wanted.

"Well, we might as well get out and stretch our legs."

Eddy grabbed his hat, pushed the door open and stepped out. He had been sitting so long his tail was almost paralyzed. He fitted the Stetson that Lambert had given him for graduation to his head. It sure was hot out here.

Lambert pointed to the desert. "Guess that's him."

Eddy looked out and saw a Jeep with what looked like four people speeding toward them. He wiggled his hips and stretched his body. The Jeep was slowing down.

Gloria Drake was driving. She thought she recognized him. Damn, it was Eddy. She headed toward them making him jump back. She stopped beside him. "What you doing out here Eddy?"

He looked at her. Football workouts had strengthened his legs but her sheer beauty instigated a weakness and they trembled. "Going to do some roughnecking I reckon."

The woman sitting beside Gloria jumped out and headed for the air conditioned office. "That's Mom. She got too hot."

Eddy could see she was a beautiful woman. She looked young to be the mother of Gloria. And it had been a wonder she hadn't busted the seat of her pants when she exited the Jeep. Not that her rear end was too big, it was because those pants were a size small. No doubt about it, Eddy could plainly see where Gloria got her beauty as well as her body. Gloria turned to the back seat. "Eddy this is my dad. Daddy you remember Eddy. He was our kicker."

Thomas Drake shifted, and reached for Eddy's hand. "You done a good job for the team Eddy."

Eddy's hand was limp and sweaty. This would be the first time, that he knew of, that he ever shook hands with a real millionaire. He was anxious for the oilman to stop pumping. "Thank you sir, but I missed some important ones." He hadn't forgot that disappointing trip to the hotel with his mother.

Gloria pointed to the back seat. "That's my little pipsqueak sister Ronda. You might have noticed her over in junior high."

Thomas was getting out of the Jeep.

"Hi, Ronda."

"You sure are cute," was her reply. She was too young to relate to her social superiority.

Lambert had approached the Jeep. "Howdy Thomas," he said as he looked at the girls and tipped his hat. "Girls."

Ronda could tell her dad was ready to talk business. "You haven't forgot, have you Daddy? You told me I could drive the Jeep."

"Just a minute, Honey." He turned to Lambert. "We been up to the rig. Looks like they bout got her ready for you to jack-knife."

"Good," Lambert replied. "We're raring to go."

Thomas leaned over and retrieved his briefcase and some maps. "Run her in the hole Lambert. I need that rig up near Hobbs. Course if you run it into a pool of black down there you will be around here for a while."

"Can I drive now, Daddy?" She jumped out of the back and ran around to the driver's side.

"Come on Lambert and I will show you the geological formation." He turned to Gloria. "You go with her Honey and don't let her drive too fast."

"Want to come along Eddy," Gloria asked.

Eddy looked at Lambert.

"Go ahead Kid. We got time to kill."

Thomas looked at the girls. "You got thirty minutes. Your mother wants to go to Albuquerque shopping. Guess we will spend the night over there." Eddy jumped into the back as Gloria and Ronda exchanged places. Ronda started the motor and tried to shift without the clutch. The gears growled. "I forgot it's not automatic." She got in gear and barely missed the fence when she whipped it around.

It was a fast rough ride and Eddy, sitting in the back, had to hang on.

Ronda slowed and then stopped behind a sand dune. She

turned to her sister, "Well Gloria, aren't you going to kiss him?"

"I might," she barked. "If I do, it's my business, not yours."

"I dare you."

Gloria turned, got on her knees, and reached over the backrest. He leaned forward grasping for her. Their lips touched. The Jeep started moving slowly.

His heart sank as her tongue unexpectedly probed his mouth. He possibly might have discharged if the Jeep had not jerked to an abrupt stop.

Gloria jerked away and turned. "Dammit Ronda, what did you run into?"

"No problem, just a pile of sand." On about the third try she got it into reverse. "Don't worry, I will get us out." Then at half throttle, she buried it to the axles.

Eddy got out to observe. The situation was not good. "Guess we might have to walk back."

He reached to help Gloria down as she was saying, "Ronda, I ought to whip your little butt for this."

"Better not," the youngster offered.

"Why not?"

"I'll tell Mom what I saw you and Jimmy doing last night."

"Aw, you didn't see nothing."

"That's just what you think," and started skipping playfully back toward the nearby refinery.

"You better keep your mouth shut, Ronda."

"Okay Sis," she waved back.

Eddy had kept silent during the altercation.

"Well, we might as well get to walking." She took Eddy's hand. "Daddy can send some grunts for the Jeep."

He walked beside her, wanting to do more kissing, but couldn't find the courage to ask. "Where you going to college, Gloria?"

"Texas Tech."

He knew damn well, but asked anyway. "Where's Jimmy going?"

"He's going there too. Got a football scholarship."

He knew that. Half the people in New Mexico knew that. "Jimmy's a good quarterback." He secretly hoped he wouldn't make the team. "He'll make them a good one all right."

"He should be all right, but they are a passing team. Are you going?"

"Don't reckon I will."

"Who needs it?" She released his hand, and led the way through a mesquite grove. Eddy fell behind and was captivated watching her hips undulating beneath her white shorts. He could make out clearly the outline of her red panties beneath, but didn't realize they had worked into her crack and was worrying the hell out of her. She stopped, turned, and worked her finger up the leg of the shorts and made the proper adjustment.

Ronda was now at least fifty yards ahead.

"You haven't got a reefer, have you Eddy?"

"Naw. I ain't fooling with the stuff."

"Why?"

"Cause Dave or Lambert one would kick my butt."

She laughed. "Oh well. A cold beer will be just as good. Dad's got a small bar on the plane. We'll go by and I will sneak us one."

Eddy had rather had a cold Coke but would drink rat piss if he thought it was pleasing to Gloria. He could almost hear Lambert advising. That's high class stuff son. Too strong for your blood. But he knew he would always love her.

When they had reached the aircraft, the pilot had already started preflight instrument checks.

Thomas Drake always enjoyed his visits to his holdings, but Mrs. Drake was bitching to go. She had some shopping to do in Albuquerque.

Later that afternoon, Lambert and Eddy drove into a town near the refinery. It was typical New Mexico town but smaller than San Sonora. It had wide streets, with an assortment of older stucco, and newer brick buildings. On the outskirts were the drive-ins, motels, and in this particular town several honky-tonks.

Eddy had been hoping to stay in the newest motel but Lambert had decided to stay at the older Westward Ho. He was familiar to the fact that a cute little blond prostitute was in residence there. He was also familiar with Eddy's virginal situation, and wanted to get that corrected as soon as possible. The blond however, would be his back-up choice. His first choice, to get Eddy bred, was that big sexy Mexican gal that hung out at Big Ed's. He knew for a fact, she could teach him more about the birds and bees in thirty minutes than the blond could all night. On top of that she was cheaper.

It was sundown when they got their clothes unpacked and hit out to the Dairy Queen for another hamburger. The lights were aglow and the crickets were gathered at the front door battling for position to enter in the next wave. Eddy heard the popping as they crushed beneath his boots as he entered. They ate their hamburger hurriedly in order to get to Big Ed's before Rosita got too occupied.

Eddy was excited.

Big Ed's was a big sheet metal building just on the outskirts of town. It was big enough for a bar and a dance floor. There was a few private rooms in the back. A live western band was playing and the dancing had already started when they arrived.

Upon entering Lambert adjusted his eyes to darkness, and headed to the bar. Eddy was right on his tail.

Rosita was sitting at the end of the bar and acted real happy to see the driller. They visited quietly for a while and he slipped her a ten dollar bill and motioned for Eddy. "Go with Rosita." He didn't figure it would take her long to take care of business. "I'll meet you at the car in about thirty minutes."

Eddy eyed her up. She was a big girl, and kinda pretty.

She took his hand and led him down a dim hall toward the back. She stopped and unlocked a door on her right, reached in and flipped the light switch.

Eddy realized he shouldn't be nervous. He was a man now. But he was anyway.

She jerked him inside, and led him toward the bed. "What's your name?"

"Eddy," was his weak reply. She had a slight accent but her English was not bad.

"You are looking good Eddyboy." She kicked off her shoes and started showering his forehead and cheeks with kisses while jerking off her clothes. She moved his hands to her breast and then to her hips. "You gonna pull them boots off, Eddy? Or do it with em on."

"Leave em on I reckon."

She sat down on the bed and moved him in front of her. Sensing his inexperience she figured she would have to undress him.

Her hands were all over him. Moving. Squeezing. Then one hand was fondling his behind while the other worked at the buttons of his jeans. Eddy was so scared he was trembling all over. He thought she was feeling for his billfold. That was some of his last sheep money in there, and he sure didn't want her to get that. His mother had always told him to beware of Mexicans. They would cut you. It was a Mexican that had cut the ligaments in his granddaddy's arm in a fight over the fence building. And he had to wear it in a sling the rest of his life. Damn, he was scared. He could just see her swiping his billfold, and if he objected, her boyfriend rushing in with a big switchblade. He figured he better get the hell out of there. He felt for his billfold. It was still there. He headed for the back door still pulling up his pants. He ran to the car, rolled the windows nearly all the way up, and locked the doors. He was soaked with sweat when Lambert returned.

If at first you don't succeed, try and try again. Then if you don't succeed, quit. No use worrying your head off. That had been Lambert's philosophy. Now after returning from the rig the next day he was humping the blond at the Motel. Making good use of the twenty dollars Eddy had paid her before he chickened out. One man's loss was another man's gain. That was a good lesson for the youth to learn. He figured he was rushing him too fast and would just let nature take its course. After all, that waitress at the café they had stopped at yesterday sure seemed more interested in Eddy than she had been in him. He had left the big tip, but it had been the half-blood she had pinched on the rear-end. Maybe they would spend the night there on their next trip to San Sonora and he could get it on with her.

Lambert's car was parked just outside her window. Eddy leaned against the front fender and noticed he could see some of what was going on through the slatted blinds. He could see he was no match for Lambert. After watching a few minutes his innards were burning. He walked back to their room to hopefully relieve the pain.

5

*W*ith Lambert's constant tutoring, Eddy Gavolin learned the complexities of the monstrous drilling rig quickly, and after working only a few months for Drake Drilling Company, was qualified to work in the derrick. There as he worked precariously high above the ground, where the birds often swooped beneath him, he felt contentment in life he had never before witnessed. Or possibly it was excitement disguised as contentment. But whichever it might be, he enjoyed himself as he stood on the edge of the steel platform, throwing his body outward, and feeling the snap of the safety belt against his stomach as he latched the speeding elevator mechanism around a ninety foot stem of drill pipe.

Then in the idle hours between trips to the bottom of the hole, he would climb even higher to the crown of the derrick where he would gaze across the desert and let his thoughts and dreams run rampant through his mind. There in peaceful seclusion, except for the drone and vibration of the powerful engines below, he often would daydream of Gloria Drake.

Now the gas well had been completed. Unfortunately a couple days behind schedule, because Thomas had been in such a hurry to get the rig moved to Texas, the graveyard shift drilled too fast and twisted the pipe stem off in the hole. After an overshot extraction, and a fairly decent butt chewing from Thomas Drake, completion complete, they were now ready to move.

The rig was already shut down now and awaiting

transportation. Eddy was alone at the motel. He had spent Christmas day lonesome and bored. He had missed Lambert's companionship, since the driller had been shacked up with that red haired divorcee.

He would call Gloria, he thought. She would be home for the holidays from college, probably.

On his first attempt, he became so nervous that he hung up on the long distance operator. On his second try however, he felt calmer. Possibly because the alcohol in the can of beer he had consumed in three swallows was reacting.

"Hello," was the woman's reply from the drake mansion in San Sonora. It was probably the maid, Eddy thought to himself. A tingling sensation pulsed through him. His body trembled, as he spoke into the telephone. "Is Gloria in?"

"No, she's not," was the polite reply. "She's up at our ski resort with her father. Would you like to leave a message?"

Our! Our ski resort! Damn, he must be talking to Mrs. Drake. He became even more nervous.

"No, thank you," he replied, then hung up quickly.

He was still shaking when Lambert burst through the door.

"Hi Eddy."

"Hey Bert."

"Had breakfast yet?"

"Uh huh."

"Excited about going to Texas?"

"Not really."

"What cooled you down?"

"I duno."

Eddy was depressed, and Lambert sensed it. "C'mon now. What the hell, you ain't slipped around here and hung up on one of these split tails, have you?"

"Not around here."

"Where?"

"San Sonora."

"Who?"

"Gloria Drake." Eddy realized Lambert would probably raise old billy hell.

He did, waving his arms and cursing. Then he settled down and tried to speak frankly. "Eddy, no hard feelings, but I want to be truthful. I've got to know you. Got to love you." He paused, searching for the right words. "Dammit, Eddy, you got your sights set too high. You'll never get in her drawers. Not that they don't stink like anybody else's. It's just that they..." He couldn't think of a good explanation that wouldn't be harmful to Eddy's inferiority complex, if he had one. He couldn't figure out just how to tell the kid that a pampered young white pussy cat didn't screw around with a light brown alley cat. They might play around a little bit, but if that alley cat gets horny, that pussy's going to scoot back to her big clean house. He was being ambiguous and finally said. "Aw hell. Get your tail in that car and haul ass to San Sonora. You just be back next Saturday. We got to be in Texas first thing Monday morning. Have to start setting up the rig day after New Year's."

"She's not in San Sonora," Eddy said. "I just talked to her mother on the phone. Her and Mister Drake are at their ski resort someplace."

"Oh yeah. That's in the mountains down near Ruidoso." He walked toward the bathroom. "I gotta pee. Thomas built that four or five years ago. Just another one of his toys."

Eddy could barely hear above the loud splashing sound. "What did you say, Bert?"

Lambert looked over his shoulder. "I said it's just another one of his toys. Think he built it just so he would have a place to stash out his hides." He returned to the room, zipped his pants, and sat down. "You say you're a pretty good skier. Go down there and spend some of that money you been making. It's not far. Closer than San Sonora." He pointed. "Just don't break a leg. I'll need you in that derrick when we get to Texas."

Eddy was anxious to go, as he watched Lambert remove his billfold and retrieve a bill.

"Here, take this hundred. You might need it."

"That's okay, I got plenty."

"Dammit, take it."

"Thanks, Lambert."

"Well, what the hell you waitin on? Pack up and get your tail outta here. I'll be waiting at Molly's when you get back."

Out of respect for Lambert, Eddy had become obsessed to imitate him. His walk, his talk, his dress, and from the money he had made in the last year and a half, he had spent excessively on a custom western wardrobe. Complete with expensive handmade cowboy boots. But even though he was enthralled with his clothing, his most prized possession was the light blue Grand Prix he had just made a down payment on. He loved that car, and driving it, feeling the plush upholstery against his buttocks, made him feel secure. Equal. Surely nobody would look down on a person driving a sparkling new Grand Prix, even if they were half-assed Indian. He must be almost there.

He felt the urge, and stopped beside the road to urinate. He stepped out behind the car door, and let his vision absorb the beauty and vastness around him. From this elevation, he could look down behind him and see the white sands of New Mexico below. In front of him, but higher, were the snow capped Sacramento mountains. Surrounding him were trees. Millions of them. Tall and graceful and reaching for the sky.

A logging truck zipped by showering him with rocks, then shot on down the winding mountain road. Eddy gave him the finger.

6

There was a light snow falling, and a heavy accumulation on the ground, when Eddy pulled onto the parking lot at mid-afternoon.

The resort was a giant log and stone castle with flickering neon lights beckoning guests to The Mountain Drake Lodge. Skiing. Heated Saunas. Live Entertainment. Food and Drink.

Smoke and sparks belched from the many chimneys and curled upward into the crisp air. Moving cable lift chairs, with the occupants' skis dangling beneath, moved steadily up the mountain. And from these higher slopes the red, and black, and blue and green clad fun seekers came barrel assing down the slope. Their arms flailing in unison with their body and legs. Swaying and turning. Jumping and falling.

Even though he had skied the mountains with his mom, this was the first time Eddy had ever visited a real hi-dollar ski resort. He surmised it would sure as hell be more fun than skiing down old Nasty Butt or the mountains over in the state park. He reached into the back seat to retrieve his hat and sheep lined coat.

When he turned around, he noticed a man and woman about to get into a white Cadillac. He quickly recognized the man as Thomas Drake. His heart sank. He and Gloria might be leaving. He felt relieved however, when he saw his employer fondling the female's rear. It would not be Gloria.

The woman turned and slapped playfully at the oilman.

Eddy noticed that she was Hispanic. She was young and pretty, but he couldn't figure out why the millionaire would be fooling around with a Mexican. He didn't do that himself, and he had some Indian blood in him. Then he realized, for the first time, he was just as discriminating as his white classmates. He would have to ponder this, and make an adjustment in his thinking.

The Cadillac sped out of the snow cleared parking lot, and onto the road.

Thomas Drake had not recognized him.

It was late afternoon before Eddy finally located Gloria. She was a little high and blurted out, "I'll kiss your ass if you can beat me down the slope."

There had been time for one more fast run down the slope before darkness fell.

"What if I beat you," Eddy asked.

She grinned, "Then you'll have to kiss mine."

"I don't have my skis."

"That's no excuse. I'll get you some at the shop."

The bet was wagered.

Gloria won the race. Even if she had not been the best skier, he would have purposely let her win. The bet, even though exciting to him, had been absorbed, and he realized it. He assumed it wouldn't be mentioned again. How wrong he was.

Now they were in his room. Her ski clothes heaped on the floor. She bent forward. Hands on knees. Her smooth flawless buttocks reflecting psychedelic images created by the flickering flame in the fireplace.

She demanded he settle the bet, knowing full well he would do anything she asked.

He dropped to his knees behind her, grasped her hips and nervously but gently touched his lips to her cool smooth flesh.

She stood up and turned toward him. "You can do anything you want to, Eddy. You can look at me, feel of me, kiss me." She wanted to say something else in that regard, but decided to wait a little longer. "Just don't go all the way, Eddy. I owe that to Jimmy." She ran her fingers thru his hair. "Just don't go all the way. Okay?"

Blood was pounding through his veins. He felt they might burst. He looked up into her face.

She moved even closer.

Eddy knew he would be obedient to her. Her every command. Her every wish. Her every desire.

Gloria looked down at him. Their eyes locked. She removed a handmade Navajo silver and turquoise Thunderbird pendant from around her neck and dropped it around his. Then jerked him against her. And in seconds she witnessed a beautiful climatic ecstasy she had never witnessed with Jimmy.

He thought he would explode. He drank in her beauty, tasted her body and compromised her soul. But he loved her so dearly, and to the maximum capabilities his young heart could possibly endure.

Later they dressed and talked. Eddy had told her how desperately he loved her. Of his desire to marry her.

"Please, don't let this thing get serious, Eddy. It was great tonight, but you know it wouldn't work between us. You know... my family. Besides, there is Jimmy. We have had this thing going for a long time. You know that." She paused. "We'll be getting married pretty soon I guess."

That last remark really hurt Eddy. Dammit, he thought. Jimmy had everything going for him. Rich, and born lily white and legitimate. One of the best quarterbacks in the state, and to top all that off, he was going to marry his girl. Dammit. Dammit. Dammit. He was furiously jealous of Jimmy Muhler, because he had now tasted the love of Gloria's body and craved more. He didn't want Jimmy, or anybody else for that matter, to come between them.

Gloria could see the pain in Eddy's face, and warned. "Don't let what happened tonight get next to you, Eddy." She knew she had her life to live and he had his. And in living her life, she would not want to irritate her father by marrying one of his low echelon employees. She had always been used to having almost anything she desired, if it could be bought for money, and she wasn't interested in giving that up. She liked Eddy all right, and the things he was willing to do for her, like tonight, but realized her best interest involved Jimmy Muhler. And his family was very rich. "I had fun and I hope you had fun. And one thing for sure, I didn't get pregnant." She laughed, and squeezed his hand. "You've hardly said ten words, Eddy. Are you still working for Daddy?"

"Uh huh."

"How did you know I was up here?"

"I called your house. Your mother told me."

"Did you tell her who you were?"

"Nope."

Gloria felt relieved. Her mother would have bitched for a solid week if she had known. And if she knew they were together now, she would disown her. Her mother's choice of sons-in-law was Jimmy Muhler. She knew that. Possibly, that was one reason she was with her daddy now. To defy her mother. She enjoyed that.

"Did you come here to ski or see me?" Gloria asked and snuggled tightly against him.

"To see you."

"Remember that week it snowed and school turned out, when you and I taught Jimmy and some of the other guys to ski down Old Nasty Butte out on your place?"

"Yeah," he smiled. "That's before Jimmy got us on that hang gliding craze."

She laughed. "It's a wonder some of us didn't get killed flying on those damn kites."

"It was fun though."

He was talking more freely now, and it made Gloria feel better to see him doing so. She realized in the past, her group had used him, even looked down on him. She regretted that now. He was really a nice guy. A little brown maybe, but nice and really handsome. And he couldn't have prevented what happened in his past. She asked, "What do you like best, skiing or gliding?"

"I duno. They are both fun." He paused. "I think I would like parachuting best. I've never tried that."

She laughed, and then said. "You are a damn good skier, Ed. You would make a good instructor here at the lodge."

"I'm a roughneck."

They had been sitting on the floor. She lay down, propping her head on her elbow. Her hair cascaded to the floor. "Would you be interested in working up here?"

"I duno," he replied while dropping to the floor beside her. "I might be if you would slip off from Jimmy and come see me every once in a while."

She squeezed his hand against her stomach.

He remembered his mother. She had bought him his first skis when he was twelve. It usually didn't snow more than two or three times a year around San Sonora, but he took advantage of those times and blazed many a trail down that old butte.

Gloria knew that after tonight she might never be intimately involved with Eddy again. She never thought she would fool around with another man after she became officially married. But just in case things didn't go right...she sure did like him. And she hoped he would work here. "Well," she asked. "Would you?"

Lambert would raise hell he reckoned, but he really didn't much want to go to Texas anyway. And besides, Ruidoso would be much closer to Gloria than Texas if she decided to change her mind.

"How much can I make?" he asked.

"Lots."

"How much is lots?"

"Lots and lots if you're willing."

"Willing to do what?"

"There's a lot of rich bitches that come up here. You be nice to them and they will be nice to you. It's not what you make, but the tips that add up. All you have to do is teach them to ski and be nice." She laughed. "Be as nice to them as you were to me tonight, and you would get rich in a few months. I guarantee it."

Eddy sickened a little bit, even if she was just joking, but what the hell. If he could just make some good money, he'd do a lot of things.

"If they are old and ugly, just be nice," Gloria advised. "But you will find that a lot of them are young and pretty and got money."

"When do I start?" he asked.

"I'll talk to Daddy, and tell him to tell Johansen to hire you."

"Won't he give you a hard time if he finds out that we've been together?"

"So what," she winked. "After all, we are just friends. Right?"

"Right."

Eddy was kinda excited about being a ski instructor. "What if your daddy won't hire me?"

"He will. He knows if he doesn't do what I ask, I'll tell mother on him." She laughed again. "And if I tell mother that he went off somewhere this evening to make it with this Mexican singer up here, she'd give him holy hell for the next year. He would do anything to get out of that." She pointed to Eddy's watch. "What time is it?"

Eddy glanced at his watch. "Ten till midnight."

"Oh damn! I better get out of here. Daddy will be back anytime now." She got up. "One more thing, watch out for Johansen."

"Who's he?"

"He's your new boss." She stood up, pushed her hair over her shoulders. "He's a queer."

"A queer?"

"Yeah." She slid into her parka.

"What's a queer doing working here?"

"Daddy hired him to teach mother how to ski. He knew if he hired a queer, he wouldn't have to worry all the time about him getting in Mother's pants." She laughed. "He's been here ever since."

After Gloria had gone, Eddy stepped outside. The snow had subsided. The sky was a milky white. There were very few stars visible within it. It was really cold now, and he was in love. Gloria must know his feelings toward her now. He had expressed them physically as well as verbally. He walked over toward the clubhouse and could hear the Mariachi band playing. Their lead singer had not returned yet.

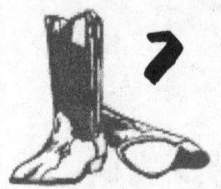

7

*S*he had come to Mountain Drake Lodge from Dallas and signed the register as Checan Martin. Real Estate had been written in under "occupation". The word "no" scribbled in under the title "Experienced Skier". She was pretty and had traveled alone to the resort. Her clothes and luggage had looked expensive. She was in room 212.

That information had cost Eddy Gavolin a five dollar tip to the desk clerk. He hoped it would be worth it.

He had been at the lodge two weeks now. Watching. Listening. Learning.

Usually it was more fun than work, except today. Today had been his day to give lessons to the children. It had been a rough day. They wouldn't be quiet. Those little snotty nosed brats had damn near run him ragged.

He was off duty now, and his head was bursting. This would be his initiation night. He listened closely to last minute instructions. Johansen assured him the woman would probably be lonesome, desiring companionship, and seeking sexual ecstasy.

Eddy was scared. Maybe he wasn't cut out for this kind of work after all.

"I'll tell you what, Eddy. If it will make you feel better, I'll go down with you and introduce you to her." Johansen sensed Eddy was uncomfortable. "Then I will slide out when the ice is broken."

"I would appreciate it, Nick," Eddy replied.

To his knowledge, Johansen was the first real honest to goodness homosexual Eddy had ever associated with. The man was tall, good looking and intellectual. You couldn't, in fact, tell by just looking that he really was one. And even though he was, when it came to money, he did not discriminate. Men or women, young or old. Eddy honestly believed the man would do anything for money.

"Are you ready?" Johansen asked.

"Yeah, let me swallow a couple of aspirin."

They walked down the open balcony to room 212. The television was blaring inside.

"I've forgotten her name, Eddy. It's something crazy." Usually he memorized a prospects name immediately, but he knew Eddy would be working this broad, and didn't bother to do so.

"Checan Martin," Eddy answered.

"Good work." Johansen laughed. "Well, let's ring this bell and see if Checan can." He paused, laughing. "Or will."

He rang the bell. The television was turned down before the door opened.

"Miss Martin."

"Yes."

"I'm Nicholas Johansen, skiing and entertainment manager here at the lodge. May we come in?"

She opened the door and both men entered. She closed it behind them.

"This is Eddy Gavolin, one of our ski instructors. Do you ski, Miss Martin?"

"No," she smiled.

"Would you like to learn?" Johansen asked.

"Yes, I would." She replied devilishly. "Are you going to teach me?"

"Well," he smiled. "All of us here at the lodge are responsible for your stay being rewarding and enjoyable. And certainly, we hope upon your return to Dallas you will consider yourself an accomplished skier."

"How did you know I was from Dallas? Mister... Mister Johansen?"

She repeated when he did not respond. "How did you know I was from Dallas, Mister Johansen?"

"I must admit, Miss Martin, I checked the register. When I saw you checking in this afternoon, your beauty so enthralled me, I just had to know where you were from."

What a line of bull, she thought. "Then you also probably saw I didn't ski." She could see right thru him. He was a good con, but not nearly as good as she. Now the dark skinned kid....

Johansen had not given her a direct answer. "Oh yes. Back to the subject of skiing, Miss Martin." He turned to Eddy. "This young man is one of our top instructors. His services will be available to you at any time." He looked at his watch. "Gosh, I didn't know it was this late. I've got a terribly important appointment at the club. Will you excuse me, Miss Martin?" He turned to the door. "Eddy can brief you on our skiing lessons. He might even give you a few free pointers tonight if you like."

"I'll bet he could," she replied.

Johansen assumed it would be almost impossible for the woman to deny herself of such an attractive young man. He liked Eddy and felt attracted to him himself, but didn't want to pursue this matter. He did not mix business and pleasure. And since he worked on a commission of profits of the lodge, as well as tips to the employees, to him Eddy was business. Good business. With his long dark hair, perfect white teeth, and light brown muscular body, he should amass a fortune from these old rich bitties if he played his cards right. His hand was on the knob when he turned and said. "If you two get hungry or thirsty while you're discussing the ski lessons, just call room service. It's on me."

He stepped out and they were alone.

Eddy looked at her. Not nearly as young, right up close, as he thought at a distance. But still pretty. Her mouth, breast, stomach, and hips were larger than Gloria's. She wore more make-up and looked more mature. His voice was wavering as he asked, "Would you like for me to leave?"

"No, let's talk. I'll enjoy your company." She pointed to a chair. "Won't you sit down?"

"Thank you."

"If you like, I will come at another time," Eddy spoke politely, his voice wavering.

"You're a fine looking guy, Eddy." She sat down beside him. "Anybody ever tell you that?"

He liked the compliment, but was too bashful to reply.

"Where are you from?"

"San Sonora."

"Where the hell is that?"

"A little desert town in Eastern New Mexico. Not far from here, on the other side of the mountains." He was twisting his fingers like trying to wring out a wet diaper.

"Oh I see." Checan had a suspicion, but now asked point blank. "Am I your first trick?"

Boy he sure felt uncomfortable now. He had heard Lambert speak of tricks, but wasn't sure this was the same thing. "I'm sorry, I don't understand."

She really believed him, but knew that Johansen dude would know what she meant. "How long have you been working here, Eddy?"

"About two weeks, I guess."

"Are you a virgin?"

Not answering, he stared at the floor.

"Tell me the truth, Eddy," she coaxed. "Please."

He stood up to leave, his head still hanging. He was ashamed and assumed she didn't want him because he was not experienced.

"Beautiful," she screamed, scaring him half to death.

She jumped up and grabbed him and hugged him, and kissed him.

"You're beautiful," she said.

He was dumbfounded. He didn't know just what was going on, and didn't much care as long as she was acting this way. Boy, was he having fun.

Checan became sexually aroused, but didn't want to rush

him. First they would talk. He was so uptight, maybe that would relax him.

She pulled him across the bed and said, "Tell me about yourself, Eddy."

"There's not much to tell."

"Well, at least I found out you've only been a ski instructor a short while. What did you do before that?"

"I worked on a drilling rig."

He was lying on his back, staring at the ceiling.

She began massaging his temples. "What did you do before that?"

Her fingers felt good. "Went to school."

"Oh," she smiled down at him. "Bet you were the most popular boy in school."

"Nope." He shut his eyes now. "Wasn't very popular."

"Why?" She unbuttoned the top of her blouse. She wished she didn't have on a bra, but at her age and size she needed it. At least it was a low cut model.

He drawled slowly. "Cause I was a bastard."

She laughed out loudly. "Aren't all high school boys bastards? At least those old maid teachers probably think so."

He opened his eyes and looked up. He was shocked to see her blouse open. "I'm a real honest to goodness bastard. I don't even know who my daddy is."

"So what, who needs them?" She unbuttoned his shirt and rubbed his chest. "Did you live in town or in the country?"

His head had almost quit hurting now. "In the country."

"On a ranch?"

"Sort of." Her big boobs were dangling just above his head. He had a compulsion to grab them. "It was a sheep ranch. Least till my mother died. After that, I sold the sheep to finish school on." He was talking and breathing faster now, trying to behave himself. "I still got the ranch though. I've always hoped someday I might drill for oil or gas and get rich. But Lambert says they ain't no oil there. He said all the oil was over on the other side of town, but they just about got it all pumped out now."

She stopped rubbing his chest and sat up. "How big is your place, Eddy?"

"Don't know for sure. Don't think momma ever did either. Guess my granddaddy is the only one who could tell for sure. Be my guess, bout six or seven sections."

She realized that would be over thirty thousand acres. "That's a big place."

"Could be another couple more. I duno."

"Acres or sections?"

"Sections."

She wondered why a family wouldn't know how much property they owned. "Why don't you know, Eddy?"

"My grandpappy and Les Smith has been fightin over some of it ever since before I was born. Grandpappy says it's his, but he ain't got no proof. Old man Smith says it belongs to him, but he ain't got proof either. It's open and he runs cows on it sometime. That didn't bother Grandpappy as long as they didn't get too close to the house and them Flying S cowboys was purty good to keeping them back. If they got by the cowboys, our dogs would run em back"

"What about the sheep?"

"We run them back up toward the mountains. More grass back there and got a mountain stream running through it."

"You sure need to know where the line is."

"You sure are right about that. But they ain't no deed to land between us and the Flying S and we can't prove it's ours."

"What happened to it?"

"Grandpappy says it disappeared from the courthouse. He figured Les Smith stole it."

"Do you think there might be any coal on your place?"

"I duno. Could be. Momma's buried in traces of it and the graveyard ain't too far."

"I'm in the real estate business in Dallas, Eddy, and down there everybody's thinking about coal. The big thing now, since the energy shortage, is lignite. Even the President says we're going to have to switch from gas to coal some day. Guess the oil situation must be pretty bad for the President to say that.

Give it some thought, Eddy." She began rubbing his chest again. "Tell you what, If you ever find out for sure that there's coal on your place, give me a call down in Dallas. I'll sell it for you." She pinched his nipple. "Since it's you, I might not even charge you a commission." She stood up, kicked out of her shoes, and slid out of her pants. Her blouse flew off as she bounced back into the bed. She couldn't remember how long it had been since her old wore out tail had so much fire in it.

Eddy felt comfortable with her. He was ready, and raring to go. He wished Lambert could be peeping through the blinds. He would be plum proud.

The mountain roads were clear. Now it was time for Checan Martin to return to Dallas. To this modern metropolis, with its glass and steel skyscrapers reaching for the heavens. Where screaming commercial and private jets flooded the sky. Their destination, the world. And below on the streets the heavy traffic, rushing like mice to get to a piece of cheese. Sirens wailing endlessly.

This was Checan Martin's city. Big and rich, and robust, and booming. Where property sold not by the acre, but by the square foot. This is where she plied her trade. In the boardrooms or bedrooms. Commercial real estate was her occupation, selling it was her game.

Her stay at Mountain Drake had been a pleasant one. She had relaxed ardently, skied with the amateurs and made love violently. She had almost forgotten the pleasure of giving one's self freely, uninhibited, no strings and no commission. But in Eddy, she sensed she had awakened a sleeping giant. It had been a pent up demon inside him that had released itself into her that first night at the lodge. A young sex starved demon. Strong and hungry.

Her bags were packed now and only minutes before they had made love. However, she could tell his enormous desires had not been completely fulfilled.

Eddy knew he still possessed an undying love for Gloria Drake, but realized that this woman before him somehow had cast a spell upon him. He wasn't sure he loved her like he did Gloria but he sure as hell knew he needed her. "Don't guess you would marry me," he asked bluntly.

She did not answer until she had walked back across the room and sat down beside him. "That's sweet of you, Eddy, but you know it wouldn't work. I'm over ten years older than you."

"That don't matter to me." At that moment, it didn't.

She knew he really didn't love her, but what she had given him instead. But that surely wasn't something that a girl his own age couldn't offer him also. All girls, in that respect at least, had been created equal. "It does to me, Eddy. I'll be getting old and gray by the time you reach your prime."

He hung his head.

"Now what I'd like to see you do, Eddy, is to leave this place in a year or two. Don't screw up your life here prostituting yourself to the women coming here for fun." She paused, and remembered from her own experience. "Believe me, Eddy, I know what I'm talking about. A person's life is too important to screw up." She took his hand and squeezed it gently. "What I would like to see you do, kick around a while, enjoy yourself, make some money. Then go back home to that ranch you been telling me about. Buy a few cows and sheep and horses. Marry one of those cute little country girls. Raise a house full of kids. That's what life is all about, Eddy."

"Then why ain't you got a house full of kids?"

"I'm different, Eddy. I started off in life on the wrong foot." Well hell, she thought she might as well tell him. "I married young, Eddy. Too young. It didn't work. After that, I considered selling myself to a select group. At first just on a part time basis. I thought I would be good at it. Really good so I considered, but backed out. I could not visualize going to bed with just anybody and I realized it would be a nasty, grueling life. I was young and pretty, went to Dallas to work for an escort service. After working a home builders convention for a few days, I decided I would like to sell houses." She looked at him. "Is this boring you, Eddy?"

He shook his head.

"Anyhow, to make a long story short, I got my license and started selling real estate." She laughed. "Damn near starved to death when I first started. It's customary to start off selling residential. Mama and the kids were always along and I usually couldn't get to Papa. That's how I learned to make it selling something besides my good looks. Later on when I got into commercial, I found that mama and the kids were never along. It was just me and Papa, and if he looked good and I couldn't sell him one way, I'd sell him the other. Now, I'm considered one of the top real estate sales people in Dallas."

Eddy didn't understand exactly all the real estate crap she had been babbling about, but she had made it perfectly clear that she was a woman of less than a reputable standing. That disappointed him some.

"You know what, Eddy?" she asked.

"No, what?"

"I'm keeping my memoirs. I'm going to write a book someday," she said. "I'll call it SEX SELLS. You want a chapter about you in there? Course, I wouldn't use your real name."

He smiled and looked at her. "Be okay I reckon, if you didn't put my picture in it."

She got up, walked to her stack of luggage, and picked up her purse. After removing an envelope from it, she returned to him, pushed it into his shirt pocket, and lightly kissed his cheek. "It's a surprise, don't open it till I'm gone."

After she had gone he anxiously tore open the envelope. His nostrils detected her recent presence. It contained ten one hundred dollar bills and her business card. He was excited about the coal business they had talked about. He would drive down to the library tomorrow, check out some books and see what the hell he could learn about it.

8

When Eddy Gavolin returned to the ranch after a long absence, there was no homecoming celebration. He had been greeted by no one. He felt a nauseous weird feeling as he entered the old home place. His eyes roamed the familiar surroundings, soaking up various objects of the past, which reflected never-to-be-forgotten memories into his soul. The mail box with its accumulation of circulars. The old barn which was still standing tall with the dusty old pickup still parked inside. Its paint rusting from the bird excretion, which had been deposited there while he was away. The cluttered house, with a broken window. And the kitchen floor, still stained with his mother's blood. It did look like somebody had been living there while he was gone. And that damn fence, recently built. Straight and taunt. Its new barbs defying animal or human contact. It now divided the sheep ranch and the Flying S. Seeing that fence had really pissed him off. Nevertheless, this is what awaited him when he returned to San Sonora.

But nearly a year had passed while he was away. And as time passed, a thing either passed with it or it had not yet come into being. But all people and all existent things moved with time.

Yet as time passed now, his memories still lingered on. The memories of his mother...and Gloria. Of Checan, and all the other women at the lodge. Not so many, he couldn't remember all their names. But to his mother, his first true love had been expressed. To Gloria, his last. He had telephoned her immediately after reaching San Sonora. She had been home from college for the weekend, but she had been very cold toward him. She seemed worried and was crying. He wanted to see her but realized at the present that would not be feasible.

He remembered the evening he had spent with her at the lodge. She had been soft and warm, yearning for his touch. She had submitted herself to him willingly, but had denied him complete fulfillment. Her perfume and the taste of her, still prevalent in his mind.

He stepped out onto the front porch, gazing across the expanse toward the Flying S headquarters. He remembered his mother. It seemed like only yesterday he had knelt beside her and promised not to let Les Smith build a fence on the ranch. He mumbled to himself, "That fence is going to have to go." He was now burning with hate inside. He needed to think. Maybe it would help if he got stoned.

The hot sun rays launched a mirage of heat waves dancing and shimmering across the desolate emptiness. The only moveable thing that seemed to shatter the almost frightening stillness was the constant rotation of the windmill propeller as it labored against an insufficient breeze to keep a small stream of clear water trickling into the near-by reservoir. Inside this tank of water, and not aware of the presence of the expensive black Mercedes which had just stopped, Eddy Gavolin slept soundly on a small inflated mattress.

The woman sitting behind the wheel was Mrs. Thomas Drake. An air of expensiveness clung like a dense cloud of smog throughout the interior of the car. From the latest hair style, which had probably been acquired from one of Albuquerque's most elaborate salons, to the blue Neiman's of a Dallas dress, which sheathed her femininity. Her slim fingers burdened and uncomfortable with expensive rings of gold and gems. However, even in the expensive attire, this middle aged woman was lovely. Even through light make-up, her beautiful face was smooth and unblemished, but drawn with anger and disillusionment. Her untanned arms and legs, soft and creamy, reflecting little exposure to the sun.

Only a few minutes had passed since she had switched off the air-conditioner, but already the late afternoon heat had engulfed the interior of the car. At first it had been just a small droplet on her forehead, but now she sensed sweat seeping from the pores over her entire body. She hated sweat. It made her smell, and certainly no woman of her stature should smell of anything other than the finest fragrance. Realizing now that some of her under garments were becoming saturated, she decided it was time to proceed with this motherly duty she felt compelled to undertake. She didn't know yet the exact words she would say to this half-breed. She would, as in the past, let her bitch temper guide her words. Possibly she wouldn't be here now if not for her uncontrollable temper. It should be Thomas here, she thought. Not her. It was not her place. She should be on the Lear enroute to Las Vegas or Dallas, or New Orleans. But Thomas, he had no guts.

Slowly she lit a cigarette with a tiny gold lighter, pushed the car door open, and stepped to the ground. Unconsciously, she moved her hands to the material which fell snugly around her hips, and gently stroked out the wrinkles which had accumulated while in a sitting position. She inhaled the burning smoke deeply, dropped the cigarette to the sun baked ground, and walked to the house. She paused at the entrance, knocked, and when nobody answered, she pulled the screen door open and stepped inside. She walked through the house, wondering if this beast really loved Gloria, or if just for his own personal pleasure, he had feasted greedily upon her youthful body. She stepped out on the back porch and looked toward the windmill.

There he was, his body naked except for a turquoise and silver pendant around his neck. Lying on his back with the raft drifting nowhere in the small metal stock watering tank. A wide brim hat with a feather in it covered his face. His body was a golden brown, long, lean and muscular. His stomach was flat, not a big round beer paunch like the one Thomas had. And not nearly as hairy as Thomas. Thomas was like an ape as far as hair on his body was concerned. She felt a surge of shame pass through her, that she was actually enjoying this situation instead of doing what she had come here to do. To give this young man a piece of her mind. It must be those hormone pills working. The ones that the doctor in Roswell had recommended. She had been losing interest lately and realized very well if Thomas couldn't be satisfied in her, he would only wander off to someone else. She didn't want that to happen, even though she had a suspicion on occasions that he had.

She felt sweat oozing from her face and thighs as she returned to the back screen door, opened it, and slammed it shut loudly in an effort to awaken him.

Eddy Gavolin stirred, opened his eyes and looked toward the house. When he saw her, his impulses responded quickly, and like a serpent, slid from the raft into the protection of the water.

Delana Drake walked to the tank. Her voice was dry. "You are Eddy, aren't you?"

"Yeah, I'm Eddy," he sputtered. His head had gone under when he rolled off the raft. He was wiping his eyes furiously. "Who the hell are you?" He could tell he was still a little tight. "Do you make a habit of slipping up on undressed men?"

"No, not really a habit of mine," came her reply. "And I don't consider you hardly a man, yet. I'm old enough to be your mother."

He could smell the fragrance of her perfume.

"You might be old enough to be my mother, but you ain't, and if you're selling insurance or pictures, or encyclopedias, I ain't interested."

"I'm not selling anything, kid."

"Don't call me kid," he demanded. "Who the hell are you anyway?" Through his memory, a sudden image projected itself upon a make-shift screen located deep within his mind. An image of the Drake Gas Refinery in Eastern New Mexico. A company Jeep with Gloria driving, and Thomas Drake slumped in the back seat puffing that foul smelling cigar, and Gloria's younger sister, he couldn't remember her name. Then this same woman, who was facing him now was, without a doubt the other occupant of the Jeep. But why, he asked himself, had she journeyed from her fashionable San Sonora home to visit him. Unanswered questions raced through his mind.

She noted the change of expression on his face and realized he had finally recognized her. "Yes, I'm Mrs. Drake, Gloria's mother."

The youth remained silent.

She watched the stream of smoke from the cigarette she had just lit fade into the sultry air. "I have only seen you once, that was at my husband's refinery."

He could well remember that day.

She waited for a reply, but after receiving none, asked, "I guess you are wondering why I'm here, aren't you?"

"Yes ma'am," he replied weakly.

"No use beating around the bush. Gloria is pregnant, and it's your fault."

At her remark, his body jerked slightly, then grew tense. If it had been true it surely would be fine. He opened his mouth to speak, but no words came out. Minutes passed as they both stood staring awkwardly at one another. Each wondering what the other might be thinking. The incident at the lodge flashed through his mind. He mumbled, "Crap."

"What did you say?"

"I said crap."

A temper tantrum was building inside her now. She could feel the words forming. "I just want to ask you one thing before I tell you what I think of you. Did you love her?"

He nodded.

An amazing transformation took place in Delana Drake's eyes. Minutes before they had been a blue green, but now the blueness had drained from them until now they were a beady solid green. "You must be pretty damn sorry, kid, to take advantage of Gloria."

He interrupted. "Now wait just a minute." Blood surged, instead of flowing through his veins. "Now let's get this straight, Missus Drake. I ain't saying that I ain't pretty damn sorry. No, I wouldn't go so far as to say that, but I will say one thing though. I didn't get Gloria pregnant. Now if you know what is good for you, you'll get your butt in that big fancy car and get outta here."

Her cheeks were red and taunt. "Don't smart talk me, you lying bastard."

He inched toward her. His voice wavering. That damn fence had already put him in a bad mood. This was almost more than he could take. "Don't ever call me that again."

After faking a hateful laugh, she replied. "What could you do about it if I did?"

"I won't do nothing if you just get in your car and leave." She calmly stepped closer to the tank, and with all the strength bent forward and slapped him. "If Gloria said you got her pregnant, then you got her pregnant. I say you are a lying sonofabitch if you say you didn't."

Eddy was surprised at the power behind the blow. He felt a burning sensation suddenly appear beneath the skin of his cheek. Slowly, his body moved upward until he was in a standing position. Modesty was forgotten, as droplets of water cascaded down his naked body.

Perhaps if she had turned and moved toward her car, he would have done nothing, but she stood motionless daring him. His powerful arms encircled her body and he jerked her harshly into the tank.

She could feel the cool water swishing against her legs. Her dress tail floated upward.

"I didn't do it," he said before pressing his lips against hers.

He could be telling the truth, she thought. Gloria was wanting to have an abortion, and she and Thomas were dead set against it. It was just possible that if Gloria mentioned Eddy was the father, they might agree to it. That conniving little... She could feel the downward exertion as he pulled her deeper into the water. At first her body rejected the pressure, but then her legs gave way to the strain and she realized that it was not his weight pulling her downward, but instead the sinful burden of desire within her soul. She could hear the gurgling of trapped air bubbles rising to the surface and could feel the cold steel of the shallow bottom against her rear.

Then after a long and grueling fight with her clinging wet panty hose, they entered into, seemingly another world.

The hormone pills were definitely harmonizing.

And after their world collapsed, her body trembled. Her lips torn within, the sickening taste of fresh blood, and the throbbing of her heart as it pumped forth, replenishing her expired energy. Her voice a different voice, so shrill that he could barely detect her words.

Perhaps she mentioned the fact that the sun had almost gone down.

The night was a thing of beauty, with the moon and stars casting shimmering spears of light toward the earth. A thing of nature, with the now crisp desert breeze blowing in the fresh pure smell of thousands of acres of densely populated range land. Possibly even primeval, as they watched the golden glow of the open fire in the fireplace, and listened to the lonesome and eerie howls of the coyote.

He was happy that he had gone to town and bought cleaning supplies and given the house a decent cleaning.

He was dressed only in his pants now, and she wore his shirt. It had a long tail and covered her adequately.

They had not talked much. Eddy's mind had been a turmoil of confusion. "I guess maybe I owe you an apology, Missus Drake."

"Don't you think you should call me Delana instead of Missus Drake?"

"Look, I'm sorry if I forced you. I was a little high."

She interrupted. "I'll admit that's not the reason I came out here." She knew that she had come to get a piece of his tail, but not in that respect. "Look Eddy, I've got an uncontrollable temper. I've said some pretty bad things about you. Maybe I'm the one that should apologize. But after Gloria told me it was you, I just couldn't stand it any longer."

"I don't know why Gloria would tell you that."

"I think I do, but I won't go into details." She felt of her clothes. They were not quite dry. "Let's just forget everything that happened, okay?"

He knew he would never forget, but agreed.

She pointed to the Navajo pendant around his neck. "Gloria used to have a necklace like that."

He touched it and remembered. "Gloria gave it to me at the lodge." He felt now, since they had been so personal there, he could share his true feelings for Gloria. "I love your daughter very much, Missus Drake. I've loved her since I first saw her in high school. And I'll love her always. Till the day I die."

She almost pitied him, knowing he loved someone so desperately, but realized he could not possess her daughter. At least not now. Not after Jimmy Muhler had planted his seed in her. Now he could just harvest his own crop. She would see to that. One thing for sure, there wasn't going to be an abortion. There was going to be a marriage. She wasn't excited about a shotgun wedding, but if need be, she would load a shotgun on the Lear for her trip to Lubbock to talk with Jimmy tomorrow. And on top of that, she might just haul his mother's big ass up there too. That would really make him squirm.

"Why did you come back to the ranch?" she asked after the silence.

"I duno," he lied. He knew damned well why he had come back. To drill for coal. And that was one area of the energy industry Thomas Drake was not fooling with. He probably hadn't thought of it, and he would just as soon keep it that way. "Just wanted to see the place I reckon."

She felt of her clothes again. They were now dry. She began dressing. She should feel guilty for the wrongdoing she had instigated, but actually had enjoyed it. And it was not like Thomas had never screwed around.

And Eddy had enjoyed also, but was already thinking about that damn fence. And like a bolt of lightning hitting his brain, he remembered the county road grader sitting there by the gate when he drove through the gate.

9

*W*hen he had turned in and headed down the white rock road toward the ranch house, he had barely noticed the county's road grader parked near his gate. He should have been happy to see his old home place, but instead, was furious when he had seen the fence. His first inclination was to wheel the car around, head over to the Flying S, and whip the old man's hairy ass. But after some serious thought, he figured to whup the old son-of-a-bitch, he would have had to go through two or three of his cowboys to get to him. And he was positively positive the time he had spent in the stock tank with Delana Drake was more enjoyable than nursing wounds inflicted by the old man's ranch hands.

He could see her tail lights disappearing down the county road just as the beam of his headlights hit the big machine. What he contemplated on doing would undoubtedly be a wild and daring stunt. But if he could start the damn thing, it sure as hell would be possible. And it sure did look like the same kind of machine he had cleared snow off the road leading to the lodge.

He removed a flashlight from the glove box, and stepped out. He walked boldly to the monster, and climbed aboard. He shined the flashlight on the instrument panel. Damn. He couldn't believe his own eyes. It was just like the one he operated at the lodge. He took a deep breath, pushed a button, flipped a switch, waited a few seconds and hit the starter. As the motor roared, black smoke belched into the desert air.

Eddy felt a great joy, stood up, and raised his arms to the heaven above. Grandpappy Gavolin must surely be smiling down on him. He was young back then, but could still vividly remember the old man dressed in black. The tall black scuffed cowboy boots with black pants stuffed down in them. The black suit coat and bow tie. And that tall black wide brim Tom Mix hat. And all that black, accented by a white shirt and a white cotton sling. His arm had been rendered almost useless by the knife wound, but strength in his shoulder along with the sling, made a good carrying place for his old worn Bible. Eddy could remember the forty-five he usually carried in a shoulder holster concealed beneath his coat. He wondered if the sinners in his congregation would have felt a little uncomfortable if they had known what the preacher was packing.

The youth lowered his arms and remembered asking his granddaddy about the gun. He said they were some mean people out there on the road when he was preaching the circuit and he didn't want to get robbed. But he said he would pray before he shot. He admitted to Eddy he was praying for the Mexican as he severed his arm. Eddy had asked if he shot him. "Yep." He asked if he killed him. "Not that I know of." End of subject.

He looked to the heavens again. He knew his mother would be standing beside his grandpappy. He couldn't see them but apologized, "You told me not to let him build it, but he done it while I was gone." He pushed the grader into gear, and pulled back on the throttle. It surged forward and over the noise of the roaring diesel engine, "It's going down Mom."

It was a still and warm night. In this secluded area of New Mexico unusual noises, which stood out above the normal sounds of the wildlife, could be heard for miles. Big Dan Silvercloud heard it, unusual noises he had not heard since his last firefight in Vietnam. It was coming from over toward the Gavolin ranch, and sounded like Hueys coming into the L.Z. while small arms fire was going out. He slipped out of bed, dressed, and hurried to the barn to saddle his cow horse.

With keen eyes he loped his mount through the moonlit

landscape to where the commotion seemed to be coming from, then dismounted and slithered through the underbrush to get closer. The destruction of the fence had been completed. Broken post and barbed wire lay strewn across the desert floor. The big road grader was parked out on the county road. It was quiet now as the operator climbed down off the machine. As the figure moved back toward the car, he recognized his son, Eddy Gavolin. His mind and heart became clogged with memories.

Dan Silvercloud mounted his horse. It would be a long slow ride back. He remembered Ruby Gavolin. From the time he had entered Big Joe's Saloon and Dance Hall in his dress blues he had been her hero. She was lonely, and he was horny. A role which would reverse itself in time, as he became more attached to her. He only had two weeks leave and would have to return to the Corps in a short period of time. He wanted desperately to spend more time with her. He wanted to come to the ranch and help out, but because of her daddy, that offer was declined. He was now the lonely one. But each third night they would meet for a short period of time, and those moments still remained a precious memory. And the last night before his departure was the most unforgettable of all. On the second, or possibly the third climax, he had run out of protection, and that evidently was the time the pregnancy had occurred.

The horse broke into a trot and he slowed him back to a walk. He wondered how Les Smith would settle the fence situation. One thing for sure, he knew he would not mention what he had seen on this night. As far as the rancher was concerned he had slept through it all. He wondered if possibly this land he was now riding on might belong to the Gavolins. After all, Ruby had told him one time the house he lived in was on her property. And he would probably trust her further than Les Smith.

And that piece of folded faded paper his mother had handed him just before he left for the Marine Corps. She had been told by Les Smith to burn it. He had carried that piece of paper in a condom to keep it waterproof while plodding through the jungles of Vietnam. And when he had returned he found out that Beauford Gavolin had shot the Mexican while he had been riding shotgun for the Flying S fence crew. He couldn't figure out why the damn place was so important to either one of them.

It was a desolate piece of worthless desert to both of them, as near as Dan Silvercloud could tell. Sure didn't seem like it would be worth fighting for.

The Gavolin dogs were trained not to let the sheep wander out on it. And since there was no water, the Flying S cattle couldn't stay out there long. Occasionally they would try to cross over and sneak a drink from the Gavolin's windmill. They would be turned away by the dogs and then have to walk all the way back across to the Flying S for water.

However, it was a haven for the Southeast New Mexico Rattlesnake Hunters Association. It was a prime location for their annual hunt, and neither Les Smith nor the Gavolin family had ever objected to their hunting there. The clean white meat of the reptile was considered a rare delicacy to some people's taste buds. That along with the abundant supply of mountain oysters available on the Flying S. Occasionally the chef at the Drake Hotel would contact him and place an order. The pay was good and the cowboys were happy to oblige. Personally, he had not acquired a taste for either. He looked at his watch. It would be a long time till sunup. Sleep would elude him.

Dan Silvercloud's mind and soul had been full of a lot of memories since he had enlisted in the Marines. He had entered the Corps as a young cowboy, born on the Flying S. He exited as a man. That had been his intention. But he had not realized the pain he would encounter seeing his fellowmen wounded and dying in the jungles of Vietnam. He had returned a hero but the stripes and medals seemed to have little meaning to him because they had been received in, what seemed to him, such a useless war. However, he considered the sacrifices of the men in uniform admirable, but the decisions of Washington politicos had been questionable. And those damn draft dodgers and protestors ... and the remnants of them still remained. His own daughter protesting and rejecting his authority while getting involved in drugs. He couldn't figure out why she could not have turned out like her older brother Damond. He had worked hard in high school, played football and had received a scholarship at West Texas State. And fortunately for him, Mrs. Dora Smith had left enough money to his wife that they could send all their children to college. But Sonya got mixed up with the wrong crowd in high school and got hooked on drugs.

He had sent her away to Brother Rob's Rehab and that seemed to have helped for a short period of time. But then she ran away from home. She said the reason was, "You are all time kissing Les Smith's ass." It sure didn't seem possible that could happen to a tough old disciplined ex-marine like himself. And now, his son had just destroyed his employer's fence. Unfortunately, if there was a fence standing now, he sure would be astraddle of it.

When Dan Silvercloud was discharged and returned to the Flying S he was quickly promoted to assistant foreman. Several reasons perhaps. His hero status, his abilities of protecting Old Les in the event of an altercation. And the fact it was about time to put the Hooch And Pooch out to pasture. They had done him and Miss Dora a good job but Les had felt it would be a prestigious event for the Flying S to have a foreman who had so many articles written about him. Dan realized his mother had saved everything she could get her hands on and had packed them away in a trunk for the grandkids. He also realized the articles didn't buy groceries or make car payments. He figured a good many of the newspapers the articles were written in, ended up in the pit of rural outhouses. At least someone had got some practical use out of them.

But now his job, as well as several others in the Silvercloud family, would be in a precarious situation if a document his mother had ordered burned showed up after all these years. And he firmly suspected it was a deed to Gavolin property. One thing for sure, he had toted it to hell and back in that rubber.

He would ride by tonight and make sure the rock was still there where he had buried the condom when he had returned to the Flying S. And next to that rock was a larger rock. And according to his Uncle Dave, who had been running the fence crew that day, was where the Mexican was buried. Les had sent him there to run Beauford Gavolin off the fence line. He assured him the old man was a preacher and not a violent person. "Take his carbine away from him, cut him a little if you have to, but don't kill him. Just scare him off."

According to Uncle Dave, the Mexican thought he was a 'bad ass'. He did not have a good day that day, but fortunately he did get prayed for before he met his maker. He successfully jerked the carbine from the old man's hands, threw it to the ground and stomped it into the sand. He then flipped his switch blade open, and moved toward him. Beauford didn't back up. He prayed instead. The Mexican slashed at his arm and bloody ligaments spilled out. He quit praying and unbuttoned his coat. He slid the forty five out of the shoulder holster and then calmly shot the Mexican.

Beauford Gavolin then picked up his carbine with his one good hand, slid it into the saddle holster, and mounted his horse. And much to the astonishment of the fence crew, and with blood dripping from the wound, he spurred the animal and rode off.

Dave Silvercloud had checked the Mexican's pulse. He was a goner. He left the fence crew behind and rushed back to the ranch house to tell Les Smith.

Les didn't bother to ride back to the fence with him. He just gave the order, "Bury him and come on back. Tell the men to never say a word about it."

Dan Silvercloud's conscience was gnawing at his mind. He knew he would soon have to dig that jar up. He would have to untie that rubber and see for sure what was in it. If it was a deed to Gavolin property he would feel obligated to give it to his son. Then when Les Smith found out, all hell would break loose.

 **10**

*S*an Sonora lay in the Great Plains Region of Eastern New Mexico. A quiet peaceful town nestled in the semi-arid desert just beyond the foothills of the Sacramento mountains. But not a large town compared to Santa Fe, Albuquerque, or even Roswell. Its population consisted of some twenty thousand thriving souls, most of whom were white. But like many Southwestern towns, residing there was a bountiful supply of Mexicans, Indians, and few Blacks.

It was a prosperous town, served by an interstate highway and A.T.&S. Railway. In the old days, a hub for the area's timber, sheep and cattle production. Several miles outside of town the tracks were the property line down one side of the Gavolin Ranch. A dilapidated sheep corral still existed there on the tracks. A remembrance of a more ambitious and prosperous time.

San Sonora was an industrious town with several small factories, the largest of which was the Muhler Aircraft Corporation. They manufactured a popular single engine aircraft. Chet Muhler had moved the plant there from up north because of employee availability and more suitable weather conditions.

The streets were wide, the buildings well-kept, and no unreasonable slum district existed. The tallest building was the Drake Hotel. Eddy could well remember his bad experience there. The newest was San Sonora State Bank. That was his destination.

He parked his car on the sidewalk just down from the bank and leaned against the fender contemplating his financial situation. Two young shoppers clad in shorts and strapless blouses were approaching. One nodded over her shoulder and he heard her say. "That old bald headed Jew must be a pervert, the way he stared at us. Jezze, you think he never saw a woman before." Eddy looked across the street.

The storekeeper was unbuttoning his expensive coat with one hand, wiping his brow with the other. It was not unusual for storekeepers to stand out front watching passers-by. Sometime smoking, sometime visiting, sometime watching. And sometime on a windy day, they might get lucky. A puff of wind might connect with a young woman's skirt and lift it upward as they were passing. If the passerby was old or fat the storekeeper would look the opposite direction.

Eddy glanced at the two women approaching him. One, for sure, wore a wedding ring. Their exposed skin was tanned. He wondered why they would be so foolish to let the sun purposely discolor their skin. He visualized the whiteness of their skin unexposed beneath their brief attire. He pictured himself hunkered in the belly of the nearest woman. A small unborn naked creature, sustained by cord from her body until he would exit from her womb, healthy and without the slightest trace of Indian blood.

"He's still looking," as they passed in front of him.

Eddy's suspicion was that they enjoyed the attention. They just needed something to bitch about. He dreaded it but didn't have another choice that he knew of. It was a short distance to Eddy's destination. He glanced up. CITIZEN'S STATE BANK OF SAN SONORA, NEW MEXICO. He had rather had his butt kicked but eased inside. It was cold. Kind of reminded him of a morgue. Not so only because of the cold, but because of some of the stiff looking light skinned employees. The men wearing suits, broad ties, and sporting clean shaven faces. The women, every hair in place, make-up, heels and all girdled up. Some sure looked casket ready to him. And he figured it was a sure bet, none of the women ever waited tables, or none the men ever worked on a rig.

Eddy didn't know exactly where to go. He eased over to a window marked LOANS, because that was the only reason he was here. He stood back courteously and watched as other customers rushed in front of him. He was in no particular hurry but wondered if his Indian blood might be showing. The window became vacant and he stepped up to it. He removed his Stetson.

A silver gray-haired lady asked. "Can I help you, young man?"

"I'd like to see about gittin a loan?"

"This is loans payable, young man." She nodded toward the front. "If you want to negotiate a loan you will have to see one of the officers."

He was a little irritated. "Which is the officers?"

She pointed at a desk toward the front. "Check with the lady at the front desk." He was getting more irritated as he turned and headed back toward the front. He definitely knew he would have to sell his car to live on, and he desperately needed a loan to buy the rig.

"Is that you Eddy," a friendly voice rang out.

He turned to the side and recognized old Jake Wilson.

"Come on in here, son." The old man motioned to the office door. "Hadn't seen you since your mother's funeral."

The office was spacious and expensively furnished, but Jake Wilson deserved such an office. He was a good banker, and being a bachelor, had devoted his life to the bank. He was intelligent and kept up with current events around the world as well as in San Sonora. He knew what was happening on Wall Street as well as Main Street. He prided himself with knowing practically every individual in town as well as most of the county residents. He belonged to every organization around, as well as being a member of First Baptist, the largest church in town. In the Caucasian persuasion of the community he was usually familiar with any pregnancy, impotency, tonsillectomy, vasectomy, venereal disease, or extramarital affair. After shaking hands he stepped behind his huge desk and motioned for Eddy to be seated. "Heard you was back in town."

"Hadn't been back long."

"Thought you might be in jail."

"Why's that?"

"Les Smith's been bitchin cause you tore some of his fence down."

"He shouldn't bitch about that. It was on my property."

"Les has got to have something to gripe about." He paused. "You knew Missus Dora passed while you've been gone?"

Eddy didn't know that.

"Got him a pretty young one roped already. One of them playgirls from out West. Heard she posed naked in one of them girly magazines." He knew that for a fact. He had the magazine. "I've seen her around town. She's a real looker." Jake didn't particularly like the old rancher because he kept most of his money in a bank over in Carlsbad. "Course you know she married him for his money." He chuckled. "She sure has got him by the yang yang. As tight as the old coot is, he had her a new air conditioned horse barn built. Guess she loves his money and his horses."

Eddy wasn't too fascinated about Les Smith's young woman. He wanted to talk money.

"Word got out, Old Les came in one day from a trip out of town, and caught her and a car salesman passed out drunk and naked on a saddle blanket in that new hoss barn. He rustled up his bullwhip, and one of them steak branding irons." He chuckled. "The salesman grabbed his keys and drawers and ran out the door. Old Les had his Indian catch him before he got to the car. When he caught em, he told the Indian to let em go. Then whupped up on that naked rump while he was unlocking the door."

Eddy grinned, figuring the salesman had a real easy time inserting his key in the slot when he was laying on that horse blanket. But it would have really been tough trying to insert it into that car door with Les Smith popping him on the ass with that bullwhip.

"That's not the worst of it. When he got back to the barn his little lady was still out. He plugged his steak branding iron in. When it got good and red, he branded his young thing right on her rear end."

"That's kinda hard to believe."

76

"Reckon it's true all right. The salesman returned to town in that fancy new sports car he was going to sell her ... in his drawers. And the doctor went out to the ranch to treat her for a burn." He looked across the desk at the youth. "It's good to see you Eddy, What can I do for you?"

"I sure do need me a loan."

The old banker reached for his pen. "I recon that could be arranged. Be like old times. I've loaned your granddaddy many a dollar back in the old days. Biggest sheep rancher in these parts before he got his arm messed up. After that he slowed down some. Done more preaching than ranching but he didn't preach for money. Left you and your mom in decent shape I recon."

"Mom wasted a lot on Lester." Eddy hung his head. "And you see where that got her."

Jake figured he better change the subject. "Say you need a few hundred to get things going since you back home?"

Eddy heard the word 'hundred' mentioned. That didn't sound good at all, but he figured he might as well get it over with. "I need seventeen thousand."

That got old Jake's attention real fast. Maybe he didn't hear correctly. "Did you say seventeen thousand dollars?"

"Yes sir."

The stunned banker asked, "How old are you, Eddy?"

"Almost twenty one."

"Why would a young man your age be needing that much money?" He paused. "Going to restock the ranch?"

"No sir, I need to buy a core drilling rig."

"What you need a core drilling rig for?"

"Want to drill for coal out on our place. Lignite."

Old Jake shook his head in bewilderment.

Eddy sensed refusal. "Sorry to take so much of your time, Mister Wilson."

Jake studied the youth's face before asking. "Think you can buy one for seventeen thousand?"

"No sir. It's going to cost more like twenty, but I'm selling my car, and I saved a few dollars."

Got anything to mortgage?"

"No sir."

"The ranch?"

"Didn't really want to do that, but the rig is a real good buy. If I don't hit nothing I should be able to sell it."

Old Jake knew Eddy didn't quite understand bank philosophy. You ain't got nothing, you can't borrow nothing. However, he did want to help the youth. "Can you operate it?"

"Yes sir." He was feeling better now. "Lambert. You know Lambert don't you?"

"He's done a little banking with us."

"He's taught me how to run a triple and that little old core rig ain't near as big and complicated."

Jake Wilson was aware of a push to convert more generating plants to coal. Possibly it was because there was so much public dissention to nuclear. People were fearful of the atomic reactors. He was also aware that some of the major oil companies were interested in investing in lignite producing properties. To his knowledge no one had bothered to explore the coal potential of this area in recent years. But he did remember when he was a kid the old timers had done some coal mining on the property which was now the Flying S. However when natural gas became readily available they abandoned the mine. He knew Eddy was interested in lignite. Strip mining. Less expensive to get to. He asked, "What would you do with it if you found it out there?"

"Sell it, sir."

"How would you ship it?"

"Same way Grandpappy shipped his sheep. Our place borders the railroad on the south. The spur is still there." He looked at old Jake. "I read that it might could be shipped in pipelines. Crush it up, mix it with water and pump it out through existing pipelines."

Jake was impressed. "Where would you get the water?"

"Drill it out. Lots of bad water in this old earth. Use the good water for irrigating the backfill."

"You been working for Thomas Drake, ain't you?"

"Yes sir."

"He know anything about what you up to?"

"No sir, his mind is mostly on oil, gas, race horses and women."

"You told anybody else?"

"No sir, nobody but a real estate lady from Dallas. It was her idea. She told me if I could find it, she could sell it."

Old Jake could remember when Thomas Drake came to San Sonora. Young, and full of piss and vinegar, and cocksure. He could well remember when he sat at his desk with the same look on his face as Eddy. He had loaned him a few thousand dollars, and with an old broken down rig, he discovered the San Sonora field up in the northern part of the county. It was not a big field but large enough to launch him into a financial opportunity that every wildcatter dreamed of. Now sitting before him, an even younger man. Full of the same piss and vinegar. He knew he couldn't turn him down. And wouldn't it be a hell-of-a-note if he loaned Thomas money to hit oil up to the north, and loaned Eddy money and he hit coal to the south. Heck, that would be a miracle. "Whoeee, I have loaned your grandaddy many a dollar in my time." He looked at Eddy. "You understand, it's going to be a personal loan from me to you?" What to hell, he had plenty of money and he sure couldn't take it with him.

Eddy Gavolin's heart throbbed. His body trembled. He was almost beyond words, but he managed a weak reply. "Thank you, sir."

The banker chuckled, "You ever get a chance, peep up your neighbor's dress tail and check out that rumor. Sure like to know if she really is wearing the Flying S brand. Just don't let old Les get you with that bullwhip." He looked at Eddy and then got serious. "How would you like to buy half the Flying S?"

Eddy smiled. "You kidding me?"

"The church owns it. Missus Smith left her half to em and they rarin to sell. They want a new auditorium and don't want to wait. I was going to buy it myself, but I'm like the Smiths. Got no kids to leave it to." He paused, opened his desk drawer, removed a contract and pushed it toward Eddy. "One problem though. Les got a lifetime estate in it and you got no control of it as long as he's still kicking. If you happen to hit on your place it sure would be nice to have. If you don't hit, you can renege on the sale." He pushed a pen and the contract across the desk.

Eddy thought he was dreaming.

11

The core drilling rig was worn, but not obsolete. Actually, it had been converted from a deep water well rig to a core rig at Eddy's insistence before the purchase had been completed. But to Eddy Gavolin, it was the most beautiful piece of machinery he had ever seen. He looked up to the crown of the derrick, and then let his vision slide slowly down to the top of the nearby windmill. To him, it resembled a proud father standing erect beside his child. Two vertical structures of steel, the tallest representing his future. The shorter, a reminder of his past. But with the taller mass of steel, which he hoped would soon be core drilling for coal, his dream stood at stake.

Soon, he knew Lambert would be departing the ranch, leaving him alone to worship this steel monster. And to Eddy, this monster was a living thing, a maze of unbreakable steel, cables and motors. A moveable thing to which he was owner and master. A thing which would work faithfully for him and not resent the endurance and punishment it would endure. A thing he would let die, he hoped, on this ranch as thankfulness for its rich reward within his life.

Eddy laughed uneasily to himself, and wondered if the things he had been thinking were normal, or just the crazy mixed up feelings of youth. He asked himself if he was normal, or if possibly his past hardships, the darkness of his skin, and his emotions had mentally upset him.

The youth's abnormal thoughts were discarded from his

mind when he was approached by Lambert Snodgrass. He looked at him. Sweat was pouring from the driller's shoulders, causing his shirt to cling to his muscled arms.

The test wells in Texas had been dry holes, and Drake pursuing a new business venture had purchased an off shore drilling rig. Lambert passing through on his way to Louisiana to operate it, had decided, fortunately for Eddy, to stop by for a visit at the ranch. He hadn't known what he was getting himself into.

The country road that ran past the ranch was well traveled, and old Jake Wilson realized that Eddy could not possibly keep the rig a secret. He recommended to Eddy to lock his gate, and purposely started the rumor that the kid was going to explore for oil up there on that old deserted sheep ranch.

Thomas Drake had gotten a particularly big laugh out of the rumor, knowing full well that he himself had punched holes all around that place. Not a damn drop of oil around there. And he knew also that Les Smith, even though there could possibly be oil on his giant ranch, wouldn't let a drilling crew set a foot on his place, come hell or high water. That eccentric old bastard was a true cowman, and if the world had to fuel their furnaces on cow-chips, that suited him just fine. And try and change his old stubborn way of thinking would be like inserting an elephant up an ant's behind. He knew because he had tried it. Even though his now deceased wife's daddy had bought him the land, he had nurtured it and had built his dream. The old man loved his land, and the thought of changing one damn thing on it, in it, or about it was out of the question.

Eddy knew this too, but he would cross that bridge when he came to it. "You about finished with that motor, Lambert?"

"Yep, guess you about ready to start drilling. You sure you understand how to jack-knife it down now?"

This was a process which would have to be exercised each time the rig was moved. The derrick telescoped downward, and then lowered vertically onto the top of its large truck.

"I can handle it," Eddy replied.

The driller removed his heavy work gloves and said, "Any more beer in the house? My throat's dry."

There was, but not much. Lambert had already started on the second six pack while working on the motor. To Eddy that was cheap experienced labor, however. He didn't know much about motors and probably could have never fixed it himself. Eddy smiled. "Your throat stays dry, don't it, Bert?"

He laughed. "A big part of the time, and my pecker stays hard a big part of the time too."

Eddy realized that.

The driller threw his arm around the youth and they walked silently to the house. Eddy pulled the screen door open and they entered. It was hot. The protection of the roof did little more than break the intensity of the blistering sun rays.

Eddy had been living in the old house several days now. He had cleaned it up, purchased a tank of butane gas, had the electricity and telephone turned on. He had bought a used window air conditioner at Sears and walked over and flipped it on. Maybe it would cool a little.

Lambert removed his safety helmet, pitched it on the table. "Whew, it's hot. Probably be hotter in Louisiana though. And them mosquitoes, damn them mosquitoes are big down there."

Eddy handed him a cold beer. He sat down, gulped and belched. "This heat makes me wish I had an office job somewhere with a cute little secretary to sit on my lap."

"I've always heard," Eddy said, "that once you're a driller, always a driller."

Lambert removed a greasy handkerchief from his back pocket and attempted to rub some of the sweat from his hands and face. "Bull. I'd quit the oil field in a minute if I had the chance."

Eddy had known that Lambert had recognized the rig as being a core drilling rig immediately. He knew too much about drilling equipment not to. But Lambert had not quizzed him about it.

He had just put on his work clothes and gone to work on the motor at Eddy's request. Eddy knew he needed his services badly, but also realized he couldn't pay for them. "Don't want to gamble do you?"

Lambert became suspicious. "What you got up your

sleeve, Indian?" He knew he probably was the only person in the world who could call him that without offending the youth.

"Wouldn't want to gamble that office and secretary against one helluva great big nothing, would you?"

He took another swallow of beer, and lit a cigarette. "I take it you are offering me a job."

"Yup."

"Working for nothing. Right?"

"Yup."

"You know me, Eddy. I gotta have my women. And no money, no funee."

Eddy interrupted. "What's your feeling toward lignite, Bert?"

"What the hell is lignite?"

"Coal."

"Oh, so that's what you are up to."

"Don't say nothing about it to Thomas."

"Screw him, I won't." Lambert tried to speak in earnest. "Look kid, all I know anything about is drilling for oil and gas. Don't know a blasted thing about coal, but in my time I've seen so many high hopes and dry holes." He paused, "I suspect I better get on down to Louisiana and get my tail to work. Then when you bust yours, I'll try and help bail your ass out."

Eddy thought that might be a pretty good idea. "Thanks, Lambert."

"By the way, I hadn't had a chance to ask you about your love life."

"Gloria got married." The words strained him.

"Who's the lucky stud?"

"Jimmy Muhler."

"Any kin to Muhler Aircraft?"

"His dad owns it."

"That stands to reason. Money attracts money."

"Yeah."

Lambert wanted to change the subject. Perk the youth up. "Did you know some of them Cajun girls down there in Louisiana where I'm going got rings around their legs."

"Naw."

"They have." Eddy was gullible, he would believe almost anything.

"Bull."

"Yeah, cause they stand out there in the edge of the swamp catching crawfish, and the water causes rings around their legs."

Being raised in New Mexico dry country, Eddy wasn't positive, but he was reasonably sure Lambert was frissin him.

Lambert looked at his watch, jumped up and said, "I've got to go." He held out his hand. "Take care of yourself, kid."

Eddy shook his hand and pointed at his head gear. "Don't forget your helmet."

"It's yours. Compliments of Drake Drilling Company." He winked as he fished several bills from his money clip and stuffed them in Eddy's shirt pocket. "Good luck, Indian."

After Lambert had gone, Eddy removed the last Sunday's edition of the San Sonora Chronicle from between his mattress and read for at least the hundredth time. GLORIA DRAKE AND JIMMY MUHLER EXCHANGE WEDDING VOWS.

Later that afternoon, Eddy Gavolin stopped by the bank to report his progress to old Jake Wilson. Then he drove directly to the sheriff's office. He had been dodging Sheriff Brinkle ever since the day he had torn down Les Smith's pretty new fence. Not that he was really worried about a complaint filed by Les Smith. He would have already had him arrested if he had proof the fence was on his property. What he was more concerned about now, was the county raising hell because he used their equipment to tear it down. Fortunately the commissioner and Dave Brinkle were brothers.

The Sheriff had not changed since the last time Eddy had seen him. A little heavier maybe.

"I wish I could say it's nice to see you back, Eddy." They shook hands.

"Aw Hell," he grabbed Eddy and hugged him. "Heard you were back. Thought you had forgot me."

"Couldn't ever forget you, Dave. You have done too much for me."

"It was my pleasure." He grinned at Eddy. "What you been up to beside tearing down fences with the county's grader?"

"Thought you might want to talk to me about that."

"I think I got you covered on that. Just don't let it happen again."

"I won't."

"How'd you find things out at the place?"

"Okay I recon. Looked like somebody been hanging out there."

"Did you see where we pulled up that field of marijuana and burned it?"

"I didn't notice that but looked like some things had been going on."

"Get my letter?"

"No sir."

"I wrote you at the lodge. Guess you had already left." The sheriff retrieved a paper from his desk drawer. "One of them young Indian gals over on the Flying S done turned kinda wild. She had problems with her parents and ran off to Brother Rob's Half Way House before she graduated." He folded his arms and leaned back. "When she came back she brought a couple of hippy druggies with her. They just kinda took over your place. Reckon she knew it was vacant so they moved in. Some of the other residents at the Half Way House would come down on weekends and they would party." He shook his head. "When I got wind of it I headed out there to run em off. They had the finest marijuana growing in that old sheep corral I ever did see. That sheep shit grew some of the prettiest stuff I ever saw. Stalks higher than your head. Least a hundred and fifty pounds stripped down. Ten dollars an ounce on the street. That's fifty four thousand dollars. Not bad, huh?"

"Beats hell outa raising sheep," Eddy said.

Sheriff Brinkle pointed to Eddy. "You don't get no ideas, hear? You got me in enough trouble already. I've brown nosed around here and got your butt out of trouble with the county, but if Les Smith presses charges against you, you know I'll probably have to lock you up back there." He motioned toward the rear.

"With them two hippies I arrested out at your place."

Eddy sure felt relieved to hear that Dave had fixed things with the county.

"Got a feeling I won't have no problem with Mister Smith."

"What's the deal on that fence, Eddy?"

"Don't know really for sure."

"If you tore my fence down, I would press charges against you. Why wouldn't Les Smith?"

"Only reason I can think of, it wasn't on his property line," Eddy said. "Maybe he built it on my property, not his."

"You just might be right." He pushed his western hat to the back of his head. "Even though he's done lots of talking, he's never officially filed a complaint with my office."

"Me and him will have to get together purty soon, and find out for sure where that property line is. Could be, the only people know for sure is him and my grandpappy. Grandpappy claimed he owned that old sorry land between us and the Flying S."

"Well, it's something you need to straighten out." The sheriff looked at Eddy and smiled. "You looking good boy. You growing right on up and you know I was just kiddin about not being glad to see you."

"Yeah, I knew you was."

"What you got on your mind? What you doing back in San Sonora besides tearing down fences?"

Eddy had been listening to the sheriff and half listening to the police receiver crackling in the background. Seemed they were talking more in numbers than words.

Now Eddy's eyes were focused on him. Pleading. He had seen that look before, and knew Eddy needed something. "Okay, what is it?"

"I need a man to help me, Dave, out at the ranch. Ain't got no money much. Even had to sell my car. Thought you might could help me find somebody."

The sheriff had gotten word that Eddy was going to explore for oil out there. He had considered it a futile effort and started to advise him so.

"Guess that's asking a lot?"

He had always felt sorry for that damn half Indian kid, and while he had stayed with him and Gin, he had learned to love him. And if he could be of assistance, why should he deny him. Of course, this would probably be cause for more brown nosing the county before it was all over with. He had the authority to do it. He could rig a release of those two long hairs on a work permit. However, he doubted Eddy would get any work out of em. Just be two warm bodies most likely. And if he didn't keep a close watch on them they would probably be out in the desert searching and harvesting peyote. And if they got all fired up on mescaline, they would hit the road, and he would have to go and chase them down. "Could you use two hippies in the place of one man?" he asked.

The sheriff had come through for him, he knew.

"It would be them two I arrested out at your place a couple of months ago." The lawman paused and remembered. "Damnest sight you ever saw. When we closed in on that old house of yours, ain't never seen so many half naked people jumping around, or heard so much screaming and hollering going on. My deputies had a real ball. We arrested two or three car loads of em. Turned em all loose though but the two I got locked up. Near as I could tell, they were the ring leaders. Wasn't no use of the county having to feed that whole passel." He stood up. "I'll go get em and let you take a look at em. After you see em, you may not want em."

The sheriff left for the cell.

Eddy was alone in the office now. There was a paperback novel on the desk. He picked it up, flipped it open and began reading. By the time the sheriff and the two prisoners had returned, he was indulged in detailed copulation of a tough private eye and his rich seductive client.

Both of the hippies were older than Eddy. They were slender bodied. Puny looking. Bushy long hair and beards. Dirty. Eddy thought he could smell them.

The sheriff wasted no time. "This here is Eddy Gavolin. He owns that place out there where you people were staying. You want to go out there and work for him? You can. If you don't, you can stay here in jail. Take your choice."

"What kind of work?" the older one asked, looking at Eddy.

Eddy closed the novel and dropped it back onto the sheriff's desk. "We're going to be drilling some holes in the ground. The work won't be hard." He sized the two. "Fellows, you probably know what it's like to be broke."

They both responded, "Yeah man."

"I'm broke. I need your help to drill. If I hit, I will make it worth your while. If I don't, all you got to lose is a little time, a little sweat."

"Anything would beat this tomb man," the younger smirked.

After the sheriff had escorted the two hippies back to their cell, he returned and said, "Gin will be glad to see you." He looked at the clock and realized his wife would probably have the evening meal started. "I'll call and tell her you are coming, Okay? It'll tickle her to death. You were her football hero. She even cheered when you missed those field goals."

Eddy remembered Ginny. The many times she had fixed his meals, and washed his clothes. He had not seen her in a long time, but realized she had been a mother to him. And this evening he would tell her how much he appreciated all the things she had done for him.

12

The two hippies from jail liked to be referred to as Butch Cassidy and Sundance Kid. They had come to New Mexico from California. And to Eddy's surprise, Butch held a Bachelor of Arts degree from UCLA. Sundance, he learned, was from a well known influential and wealthy family from Hollywood. He sure couldn't understand their motives, but had gained their friendship and realized that he liked them.

Aside from those two, Eddy also had become quite fond of Sonya Silvercloud. She had run away from home again, but this time instead of going to the Half Way House, she had just moved into the house with him and the two hippies. He didn't quite understand why her daddy would tolerate that. He did remember her from high school. She had been a couple of grades behind him. She and her brother had ridden the bus with him. Actually, his name was Damond but was nicknamed Chief by the football squad.

Chief was big, tough, and smart. A lineman, whose responsibility was keeping opponents from knocking Jimmy Muhler on his lily white butt.

Sonya had no quarrel with Chief. Her rebellious hostilities had been exercised upon her parents and family. Slavery had been abolished many years before, but she considered her parents Indian slaves, and Les Smith their white master. Her mother and grandmother, in addition to raising their own families, had to do the ranch's cooking, washing, cleaning, nursing and had on several occasions even administered enemas to the late Mrs. Smith. And her father, in addition to running the Flying S, was responsible for Les Smith's personal safety. Being a body guard wasn't so bad, but being ordered to hold that poor salesman till Les Smith retrieved a bull whip was just more than Sonya could stomach.

At first it was a casual situation at the sheep ranch. One big happy family. Sonya, the shapely young Indian, cleaned the house, made the beds, and arranged the two-a-day meals. She was kind, and unselfish.

Aside from their drug habit, shabby looks, and bathing inadequacies, the group, to Eddy, was not half bad. They didn't cuss, didn't smoke, and didn't drink. They even seemed religious at times, and talked mostly of world peace and love. Their drug habit, however, would have no doubt bankrupted Eddy, if Sheriff Brinkle had not periodically dispensed to them a smidgen of county drug evidence he had confiscated in various arrests in the past. Eddy had promised at the sheriff's insistence, not to get hooked on the drugs. So while Sonya, Butch and Sundance partook drugs, he partook lightly in alcohol.

Eddy was surprised at the group's willingness to work, except when they were stoned. They seemed interested, responsible and had learned to operate the rig quickly. Eddy had confided in them, and told them he was drilling not for oil, but for lignite. This had really turned them on in a way. They were all ecology freaks, and they hated to see the earth scarred with strip mining, but were agreeable when Eddy told them of his dream to reclaim the soil by fertilization and irrigation and turn the desert into a green ocean of vegetation. They had really been hip to that. This talk possibly so inspired Butch and Sundance that they went down by the stream and planted another field of marijuana.

Work was progressing smoothly now. With colored markers, Butch had detailed a map of the area on a poster board. He had used as reference an aerial photograph found in an old cedar chest, and at the request of Eddy, had included most of the land to the Flying S Ranch. Each drilling location had been noted on the map as well as the depth of the lignite. At the back of the place, over near the federal lands, coal depth was zip. At the stream and timber, three to four feet. Too shallow to mine profitably. One half mile east of the timber, thirty foot vein, sixty feet deep. Profitable. Near the butte, seventy foot deep. Very profitable. Just behind the old ranch house, eighty foot deep. Unbelievable. Out front of the house toward the Flying S, over eighty feet deep. The vein was, no doubt, increasing in depth toward the Flying S. He gazed across the desolation. It was time to confront the old bastard. The rig had lights on it, and they had been working violently day and night. Usually in shifts with Sonya delivering ice, water, baloney sandwiches, Vienna sausage, and sardines to the rig in the old pickup. Eddy didn't like sardines, and on that day he made do on peanut butter and crackers.

Eddy realized that right under Thomas Drake's nose he had discovered one of the biggest veins of lignite in New Mexico. Enough coal under the sheep ranch alone that he could no doubt live comfortably the rest of his life. And in doing so, he wanted to share at least part of his success with his three friends. His first ambition was to get Sonya in a good hospital somewhere and see to it that she kicked her drug habit. He would even do the same for Butch and Sundance, but doubted they would be willing. They were pretty hung up on drugs, but not really more than Eddy was becoming toward Sonya. When high, they talked of non-violence, sharing, peace and love, and a bunch more crap that Eddy couldn't hardly relate to. What he could relate to, though, was his feelings toward Sonya. Not a fiery burning love like he possessed for Gloria Drake, but a deeper warmer feeling of attachment. He could feel that same feeling resonating from her. She was busting her butt to please him. But he was growing more irritated and disgusted, not necessarily at Butch and Sundance, but at himself. They had worked hard for him, but he was growing insanely jealous of the fact that Sonya was sharing herself with them. He was considering sending her away, back to the Half Way House maybe. But down deep, he knew things wouldn't be different. There would be others for her to share herself with. The hippy way, "live free."

The world was cruel and harsh Eddy knew, but Sonya was

not. In the community, he knew she was considered an outcast, a dope head, and a whore. But she was kind, understanding and had adopted a stray kitten. Perhaps there should be more outcasts like Sonya Silvercloud. Maybe the world would be a better place to survive. But what the hell, he had other things to worry about. Today he would challenge Les Smith.

He had hired a bulldozer to cut a primitive road through the desert to about three-fourths distance to the Smith ranch house. It had been a perilous task getting the truck and the rig through the mesquites, across the gorges, and around the rocks to this almost inaccessible location. It had been grueling and hard work. Finally completed, they spotted the rig within an area visible from the old rancher's bedroom, and raised the derrick. It loomed above the green mesquites like a ship's mast above the sea.

Eddy figured they would be having visitors soon. "Sundance, I know it will be hot up there, but how about climbing up that derrick and hollering if you see anybody coming."

"Who are you expecting, man?"

"Les Smith, probably." Eddy had wanted to bring the old shotgun, the one that was kept behind the seat of the old pickup, but Sonya wouldn't let him. She was really far out when it came to guns and violence. Eddy grinned. "I ain't really sure if we're on his place or my place."

Sonya's cat jumped from her arms and headed for the rig. She caught it before it got there.

"Hey man." Sundance was shocked. "We not going to have a range war, are we?"

"Naw, Les Smith ain't got nothing against you and Butch." Eddy wiped the sweat off his brow. "Worse he can do is make us move the rig." Eddy figured if the rancher really owned the property the rig was on, he wouldn't come immediately. He would go get Dave Brinkle first. But if he was bluffing, he'd get his old tail over here in a hurry and start blowing off a bunch of steam.

Les Smith was old and peculiar, but he still appreciated pretty things. Unfortunately, his first "missus" as he called her, got old and sickly and he had to take his beauty in on mostly his cows and horses. But after her death he had latched onto that pretty young stripper down in El Paso known as Peaches. And even though he was considered a tightwad, when it came to something that was pleasant to his somewhat fading eyesight, no expense was barred. Animal or human. He had stocked her wardrobe with an array of exotic gowns, lingerie, and western outfits and bought her a fine horse. He had even gone so far as to pay $2,000 for a videotape machine in order to record the "big event."

And possibly, besides getting rid of that half-breed kid down the road, his most treasured ambition was to ride beside her in the Rose Bowl Parade. On two matched Palominos with black leather saddles inlaid with silver and turquoise. Right there on national television, for the world to see.

Les Smith had looked over all of New Mexico and half of Texas before finding a gentle Palomino gelding matching his own. He found one in Fort Worth, and gladly paid the $30,000 asking price. Today was the first day she had ridden him. Shore a purty sight he thought to himself, as she loped the magnificent animal around in the corral.

"Mister Smith. Mister Smith," the Indian boy was hollering. His skinny brown arms waving. Barefooted. His clothes a little thread-bare from playing.

The rancher thought the kid must have seen a rattler. "What's wrong with you, boy?"

The youth was gesturing toward the desert. Too out of breath to talk.

Les Smith looked out toward where the boy's bony arm was pointing. And then he saw it. The derrick. A white flag flying from the top.

Sundance had wanted peace, not war.

The rancher got so mad he was afraid he might suffer another heart attack. His horse was already saddled. So was Dan Silvercloud's. He knew that in the pickup, they would have to go around. On horseback, they could go straight to the derrick. He walked over to his pickup and jerked a carbine off the rack and retrieved his bull whip. He just might whip the piss outa that smart ass half-breed for standing up to a man of his caliber.

Fifteen minutes later, Eddy could hear Sundance shouting above the roar of the motor, but couldn't understand him. He shut it off because he figured that would be Les Smith coming. He looked up and saw the young hippy pointing toward the Flying S. He heard him holler. "The posse's coming, Boss."

"I figured it was about time," Eddy replied.

Butch began to hum.

Eddy recognized the tune. "High Noon."

"I can't tell for sure, man," Sundance warned. "Whether it's Kirk Douglas or John Wayne." He scurried down the steel tower, puffing. "We better get the hell out of here, man."

Eddy laughed confidently, but dropped his smile when he saw the carbine. There were three riders approaching. Two he recognized. Les Smith and Dan Silvercloud. The third he presumed to be the rancher's new wife.

They stopped their horses, eyed them good, and then dismounted.

Eddy walked toward them, checking out that carbine Les Smith was holding with the left half of his brain, and the woman with the right half.

She stood beside the prancing gelding. Her smile wicked. The sun reflecting upon perfect white teeth. Long black hair probably dyed, flowed from beneath a sequined red western hat. Her shoulders poised, her back straight, causing her breasts to bulge outward. A wide leather belt buckled too tight around her waist, causing her hips to balloon instead of flow into tightly fitted riding pants. Petite white pointed high heeled boots sank into the sand.

There was a minute of silence. Les Smith had come to him, Eddy thought. He should be the first to speak.

The rancher handed the reins to the big Indian, and walked over to the woman and said. "Eddy, this here is my wife Peaches."

Eddy would have liked to have shaken her hand, but nodded and tipped his hat instead. He was busting a gut wondering if there really was a Flying S brand on her rear end.

The rancher pointed the carbine to the rig and scowled. "What's that contraption there?"

Eddy decided to tell Les Smith about the coal discovery. He would have to tell him sooner or later anyway. "I been drilling for coal, Mister Smith."

"In this country we need more water, boy. Not coal." The rancher turned to the big Indian. "Ain't that right, Dan?"

"Yes sir, we could use at least two or three more windmills around here."

The rancher cradled the carbine. "You hit any of that coal yet?"

"Probably enough to make us both rich."

"I'm already rich," he spouted. He glanced over at the woman. "Got plenty of money to tide me and Peaches over I reckon." Then looked back to Eddy. "Like I said before, with all this good grazing land around, we need water, not coal." He was just waiting for the half-breed to smart off. He was yearning to order Big Dan to grab him and hold him while he gave him a taste of his bull whip, but deep down he knew it was him, not Eddy who was trespassing. And for sure he did not realize the true situation. Dan Silvercloud would not have touched the youth.

"That's what you need, Mister Smith. Not me."

The rancher knew it would be fruitless to offer to buy the youth's property again. He pointed the rifle at the rig. "That there goldarn contraption is on my land. I want it moved off today. If it's not, I'll have my hands tear it down first thing in the morning."

Now it was time for the long awaited confrontation. Eddy warned, "I'll have the sheriff out here in the morning. You bring the deeds showing this is your property, and I will move the machine. If you don't bring the proof, I'm gonna start drilling."

Les Smith became furious. He had let the half-breed bastard outbluff him. He needed desperately to release his anger on something or somebody. Afterward, he would need to think. When younger, he would have broken the meanest horse on the Flying S to vent his fury. But at his age, all he could do was torment hell out of the meanest bull he could find. His throat was dry. His heart pumped liquid hatred into his veins. He stumbled back to his horse, mounted the animal, and spurred him hard and inhumanely. The woman and the Indian were hot on his tail. Undoubtedly he would have had that heart attack if he knew the youth had signed a contract on Missus Dora's half of the Flying S.

13

Two days had passed since the encounter with Les Smith and he had not showed up with any kind of a deed or proof of ownership. Eddy had now started drilling and was excited. He had drilled almost 60 feet and had still not bottomed out. Butch, Sundance, Sonya, and her kitten were at the rig. Drilling, pushing downward toward the bottom crust of the thick rich vein.

Eddy decided to confront the rancher once again. He would go to his house and talk to him. It was time they settled this once and for all, where the hell that property line was.

Perhaps five miles of rocky county road passed beneath the wheels of the pickup with nothing breaking the monotonous scenery except fence post, mesquite bushes, and the co-op highline which weaved endlessly to and from the few ranch houses. Just beyond where the clechie road turned into a paved road, two tall weathered posts appeared in the fence line. Lying horizontally across their tops was a sagging piece of timber. Beneath this sagging timber hung a long plank adorned with an assortment of steer horns, and the burnt lettering FLYING S RANCH. Midway down one of the upright poles, a sign read MEMBER NEW MEXICO CATTLEMENS ASSOC. Directly across on the opposite pole, another sign read LES SMITH, OWNER AND GENERAL MGR.

Eddy slowed, turning in over the cattle guard and looked beyond the large ranch house. The open rangeland looked like infinity. He glanced over at the corrals which lined the railroad spur. From here, huge quantities of beef were shipped by rail to large packing companies across the nation. Eddy dreamed that one day coal, as well as beef, would be riding those same rails. This, however, was yet to be decided.

The paint on the large two-story frame house was peeling. But it had been an original shining light and dark gray monument to Dora Smith's father who had furnished the money to build it in the early part of 1930. A hitching rail still existed near the entry. To the rear of the ranch house, past the bunk house and cook shed stood a shiny new metal barn. The Indians' houses and out houses were located a few hundred yards west toward the sheep ranch. Meager dwellings for the fifteen or so Indians serving the big ranch. With the exception of Hooch and Pooch and a few stray cowboys, Les Smith used Indian labor because they worked hard, and cheap.

Eddy stopped the pickup in front of the house, stepped out, and walked to the wide veranda. It was cool and quiet. He moved to the large stained glass door and knocked.

"Just a minute," came a voice from within.

Peaches Smith suddenly appeared in the doorway. "Hi." She smiled and pulled the heavy carved door open. "This is a pleasant surprise."

Eddy was much closer to her now than he had been at the rig. He could smell liquor on her breath and envisioned at least half a lard can of makeup on her face. Most around her eyes. She looked older. Her big breasts beneath the gown sagged more now than he had remembered at the rig. He reckoned she was not girded up now as she had been then.

He removed his hat and said, "Sorry to bother you, Missus Smith, but I was needing to speak to Mister Smith."

"Won't you come in?" she asked.

"Is Mister Smith here?"

Peaches was wearing a thin gown and with the exception of gloves and heels, was dressed in her uniform, as she called it, having earlier performed for her husband. She took his arm and jerked him inside. "Don't worry, I won't bite you."

Each morning after his breakfast at sunrise, daily toilet, and briefing with Dan Silvercloud and Hooch, the ritual occurred. Nasha Silvercloud, the housekeeper would be released from the big house to attend her own personal chores. This was the rancher's cue to return to the house for a one-man audience at Peaches' performance. She would apply loads of makeup and dress in one of her many sequined striptease outfits, replete with, heels, pasties and G-string. Then on the bar, dance and strip in tempo with the expensive and elaborate music and lighting system Les Smith had installed. Afterward, when the old rancher would leave the house, she would usually drink her breakfast. This was almost an everyday occurrence, with the exception of Sunday. On Sunday, the "odd couple" as, they were referred to by some of the congregation, attended San Sonora's First Baptist Church. But since the incident with the salesman, Les just sat in his rocker listening to a preacher on the radio. This was great for her. She would have the day off.

Peaches detested the weekday routines. She was always sleepy in the mornings, but these were two of the things she had agreed to before her vows to the rich old pooph, and about the only time she could squirm out of it was during her monthly period. These usually lasted seven to twelve days, according to her, with the old man never the wiser. These days were usually spent in bed watching television. She was getting damn tired of the ritual, but her nude modeling career had floundered when the magazine went busted. She had then moved to El Paso to take a job at a strip club, but it had turned out to be a living hell. Those soldiers at Fort Bliss were horny, but didn't tip worth a damn. And the girls over in Juarez were competitive bitches.

At least she didn't have to attend church anymore. Since the salesman was an upstanding member in the church, Les had mentioned to his wife, "Better keep your man away from my place or I will shoot his tail off." He had filled her in on the branding as well as the whipping. During the salesman's divorce proceedings the word got out, and now the old bowlegged geezer was just too embarrassed to go to church. But at least he had let her import a couple of chefs from California, and now she didn't have to eat grilled cow twice a day. And after one good look at them, Les realized they were hung up on each other and therefore he would not be jealous of them around Peaches.

With the exception of the "big night" each week about all she had to do was eat, sleep, drink, perform, and ride. And even though she was getting fed up with the performing part, everything else was working out fine. However, she was gaining a few pounds. She loved her horse but detested the old man. But if she could just stay with the demented old bastard till he bit the dust, she would be loaded. Actually, she wouldn't have a major problem with speeding the situation along a bit.

"Is Mister Smith here," he asked again, remembering the rumored episode pertaining to the car salesman.

"I'm here all by myself," she purred. "Old Nasha won't be back till this afternoon to clean, and the cooks have gone shopping. Hooch and Pooch will be watching TV in the bunkhouse and Les has gone to Artesia to buy a bull." She pushed the door shut, and led him across the entry hall to the parlor.

Eddy realized it was an architectural marvel. A large open room with a curving and graceful stairways leading to the upstairs facilities. Twin native stone fireplaces ascended opposite walls, facing an array of Victorian furniture. A long antique bar, with its polished silver dollar top, reflected the light cast downward from two old wagon wheel fixtures. The dining area consisted of several bar type tables, which doubled for both food, drink, and gambling. An assortment of longhorns and western paintings decorated the walls. The floor was a wide plank, covered with an assortment of colorful Navajo rugs.

Eddy enjoyed viewing the huge room, but figured it might be best if he got his tail outta there. He inched slowly toward the front door. "I guess I better be going."

"No." She grabbed his arm again. "I've been wanting to talk to you. In fact, if you hadn't come by, I would have tried to contact you soon anyway."

"What you need to talk to me about," he asked?

"Coal."

"That's what I needed to talk to Mister Smith about."

"Talk to me instead." She led him toward the bar. "Think there is coal here on the Flying S?"

"Yup."

"A lot?"

"Yup."

"In dollars?"

"Who knows? Millions."

That excited her. To hell with the drink. She would coax him directly upstairs to her bedroom and seduce him. And then...

"I've been trying to get Les to build me a new house and let me have some friends." She slowly eased him up the stairs. "But he's so jealous since I had that affair with that car salesman, that he won't let me around anybody."

Each step, his knees became weaker.

She laughed. "You heard about that, I guess. Everybody else has."

"I heard," he said. "Didn't pay no attention. Rumors are pretty bad in a small town like San Sonora."

"This wasn't a rumor. Les caught us. We was drunk as hell." She paused. "That big Indian grabbed that pore little man and held him till Les could get to him with his bullwhip. Les said later he wet his shorts."

"Reckon he peed on Mister Smith?"

"I hope he did. Be good enough for him. That might be the reason he told his wife. That was a big mistake."

Eddy had stopped now. Resisting.

"He held me and branded me with one of them little ole branding irons Pooch brands his steaks with."

"I can't believe that."

"Want to see it," she teased. "I'll prove it to you."

He damn well wanted to see it, but couldn't muster the courage to reply. His curiosity was bucking his common sense.

"I'll show it to you." He watched silently as she turned her back to him and began working her gown upward. When the material was above her hips, there it was. A scarred S and the familiar curving wings signifying the Flying S brand.

She was looking over her shoulder watching his reaction.

"See there. You believe me now, don't you?"

The youth stared nervously at the scar on the delicate skin of her right buttock. "That was cruel."

"I could kill him." She meant it. If she was crazy enough to marry him for his money, she was crazy enough to kill him for his money.

"Why don't you leave him?" Eddy asked.

"Money." She spelled it out, "M-o-n-e-y."

He couldn't resist. He rubbed his fingers over the scar and more. "Half of its yours I recon, you're his wife, ain't you?"

She felt his hands. She did not resist. She had him now. "If I stay with him till he dies, I get it. If I leave him, it goes to the church." She faced the youth. "Will you screw me, Eddy?" She could see that he would. She removed the tasseled pasties, and G-string.

It was a big bedroom with a high ceiling, and fading wallpaper. The furniture was massive and old. But the lighting had been modernized for a camera.

She could sense he was hot as she rubbed against him. "Do you like me, Eddy?"

He nodded.

"Really, a lot?"

He nodded again.

"You need money, don't you?"

"Yeah but..."

She interrupted. "You know that my husband hates your guts."

"That figures." He knew he'd dealt the old man much mental misery since returning to San Sonora. And His grandpappy had dealt him even more while he was alive.

"How would you like to own half the Flying S?" she asked point blank.

Eddy was shocked. He figured she didn't know the full circumstances about Mrs. Smith's half.

"Well."

He was truthful. "I would like that."

She felt confident now. Her voice was dry and greedy. "I

want to get my hands on some of the old codger's money. He may live to be a hundred. I want it now. You said yourself that coal is worth a lot, but he will never sell. Not as long as he is alive. And all these cows, thousands of them. We both could be rich."

Eddy was terribly nervous and uncomfortable. He hoped she wasn't thinking what he thought she was thinking.

"I've got it all figured out. It's perfect, Eddy." Her breathing became labored. "The bull. He's gone to the Double B Ranch near Artesia to bring back a bull. A killer bull, Eddy. The one that killed that rodeo clown last weekend. They were going to shoot the bull, but Les went to buy it. Buy it just so he could kill it himself. But in his mind, Eddy, it will be you he's killing. Not the bull. He hates your guts."

Eddy wanted to be out of there.

"You help me, Eddy. Tell him you came over." She thought for a moment. "Tell him you decided to let him build the fence back. Offer to help unload the bull. He'll be so glad to hear about the fence, he'll let you. I'll help, too. It will be after dark. We'll tell him not to bother with the hands, that we'll help him."

Sweat broke out on Eddy's face.

Her voice was husky. Almost that of a man. "The bull will be in the front compartment. When the old bastard goes into the trailer to unlock it, I'll latch the back gate. Eddy, you hit the bull in the butt with a hotshot. The bull will gore him to death."

"Woman, you are crazy."

"It will be perfect, Eddy." Her lips were dry. "Everyone will think it was an accident. That bull has already killed one man. No one will ever suspect."

Nausea swept over him. He pitied her for what she was; a scheming gold-digging harlot and a would-be murderess. The room seemed contaminated. He felt dirty.

She reached for him pressing her huge silicone injected breasts against him.

He pushed her away. "You're mad. Stark raving mad." He heard a commotion outside. Through the upstairs windows, the stench of smoke entered his nostrils.

"Smoke!" he shouted. "The house may be burning down."

She giggled. "I hope it is the house. It's nothing but a big damn shanty anyway. And on top of that, it's built out here in no man's land."

He pushed her aside and ran down the stairs. Not until he stepped into the front yard did he realize where the smoke was coming from. Billowing not into the sky, but drifting at ground level across the desert. It was his drilling rig! He bolted to where the pickup was parked.

Flames leaped violently into the sky, a light breeze blowing from the north causing dark black smoke to roll across the area toward the Flying S. He heard the earth jarring explosion, but not the scream of horror. As he sped toward the scene he could not see the steel derrick vibrating dangerously. Nor could he smell the stench of gas, flames or searing flesh.

It was a scene of devastation—unbearable heat—loud crackling noises as the flames shot upward, being fed by a continuous flow of methane gasses gurgling from the earth's guts.

Eddy Gavolin trembled in terror as he drew near. He felt sick and scared. His heart pounded. He tried a shortcut, shifted to second trying to jump a ravine. The truck stalled. He jumped out and ran. He fell. Frantically, he got to his feet and ran again. Sweat saturated his clothing. He stumbled. There was Butch and Sundance. Where the hell was Sonya?

"Where is Sonya?" he shouted. He could feel the heat now.

They were at his side. Restraining him from going closer.

"Where is Sonya," he asked again.

Sundance wanted to reply. Words clogged his throat.

He looked at Butch. "Where is she?"

"I'm sorry Eddy. She ran to the rig to get her kitten. We couldn't stop her Eddy. The propane tank blew."

The rig had been designed to run on liquified fuel instead of diesel. That had not been a problem since there was a large storage tank already on the property.

Seconds passed in silence before the stark realization sank

into the youth's mind. His body became a trembling mass. Bleary tear filled eyes. "I got to find her," he charged toward the rig.

Butch and Sundance made a futile effort to stop him.

Heat and smoke engulfed him. And then the transportable fuel tank blew. The concussion knocked him to the ground.

Les Smith returned to his ranch in mid-afternoon. He had decided to go to Carlsbad to seek legal advice instead of going to the Double B. He showed the lawyer a deed, and lied that Beauford Gavolin had lost the property to him in a poker game. The property line had been established between two steel stakes driven into the ground. One on the railroad fence, the other directly opposite on the county road. They were conveniently located at the same location that the cross-fence was being built when Beauford Gavolin shot the Mexican. And Les Smith had been the only person who had witnessed the signing of the deed.

The lawyer agreed that the deed looked all right but without a witness, or the stamp of an authorized notary, it probably would not hold up in court. He advised Les that he would try it, but that he would probably be wasting his money.

The land had become an obsession for the old rancher. Didn't look like he would be able to run the kid off. He couldn't legally prove the land was his, but nobody else could prove the land was theirs either. He had seen to that years before, when they paid a visit to the courthouse. He had located the original deed in the cavernous bowels of the old courthouse and showed it to the Mexican. Then while Les entertained the little old grey haired county employee, the Mexican with his razor sharp knife removed the original recording and slid it beneath his vest. And now, the rancher felt comfortable the deed had been burned. The half-breed sure as hell couldn't sell the coal on it if he couldn't prove it belonged to him. He would continue telling everybody the land was his, and would let his cattle run there. Even if he did lose a few head to them rattlers. And tomorrow he would go to the Double B and shoot that mean assed Brahman bull.

"Why did I have to be the one responsible for her death?" Eddy said, tears in his eyes.

Big Dan Silvercloud asked calmly, "You didn't send her in the fire did you?"

"No sir. She went after her cat."

"Why do you feel responsible?"

"She didn't have to be here. I could have sent her home."

"She would not have stayed. She felt safe and happy here."

The big Indian motioned Butch and Sundance away, as well as the vaqueros around him. His eyes were moist, his heart burdened. He spoke point blank, "I think you should know." Then out of the blue, "Eddy, I'm your father. Sonya was your half sister."

This stunned Eddy as if he had been struck by a bolt of lightning.

"I had wanted to marry your mother, Eddy, but after you were born you made her so happy she no longer seemed interested in me."

A lump formed in Eddy's dry parched throat. Goose pimples popped up beneath his sweat. He didn't know whether to respond to Dan Silvercloud with hate or love. One thing he did know, he wanted to die at this very moment. He sure would like to be up there with his mother and his grandpappy.

Coal. Formed in the earth hundreds of millions of years ago. The air was then damp and steamy. This region was covered by dense strange forest and swamp. Giant lizards as big as ships, insects as big as planes inhibited the area, and as these giant trees and ferns, lizards and insects died, they fell into the swamps to rot among their own decaying excretion. This formed peat. New vegetation grew on top of the old. Then, it too died and fell integrated into the already existing mass. The surface then sank and water flooded the area, causing sand and silt to be deposited on the layers of peat. The weight of the water compressed the peat, thus forming coal. And directly beneath this thick bed of coal, lying there ruthlessly, relentless to escape from its pressure, was the methane gas. Untapped. That is until the bit of Eddy Gavolin's core drilling rig pierced the lower crust of the coal and entered its domain. It responded by erupting violently.

Eddy had recovered now, somewhat.

Sheriff Brinkle, along with the local fire department from San Sonora had lost no time getting there. However, the firemen had already fed the flames their truck's supply of water, but it was useless. The blaze still soared.

The fire chief figured that the only probability was to blast the flame out. Hire a professional. "Read an article just last week. Man down in Houston. Goes all over the world fighting oil well fires like this."

Eddy was familiar. He had heard about him while working for Drake Oil. He charged five thousand dollars an hour. Where would he get that kind of money? Besides, this wasn't an oil field fire. This was probably just a small pocket of methane.

"You better try and get him up here," the fire chief suggested. He had already thought there might be another fire in the area. Where the rig had been located, vegetation was sparse. Grass was nonexistent. "Nothing else around here gonna burn don't look like, and we are empty. Guess we better get to town and refill our tanks." He looked at Eddy. "You call that man down in Houston. Hear?"

Eddy nodded. He had other plans.

The fire truck left, barely making it back across the rough terrain to the road.

Eddy was looking at the sheriff now, and the lawman recognized that familiar look. He began shaking his head. "Now dammit Eddy, I don't know what you are about to ask me, but I got a feeling that I'm about to turn you down."

Eddy was remembering his science teacher, Mr. Green. The times he had come to the ranch. The times he had taught himself and those crazy school kids to climb the steep side of the butte and the glider flights down the back side. And the time he had caught the teacher fooling with Nora Jean in his pickup. But most important, he remembered that time in class that Mr. Green had bragged of being knowledgeable about the components needed to produce nitroglycerin. He had even said he could produce it in the school's lab if necessary. Eddy remembered that clearly.

"Well, what is it?" The sheriff asked.

His voice was burdened and distressed. "Do me a favor, Dave. Radio one of your deputies in town. Ask him to round up Mr. Green, the high school science teacher and bring him out here."

"That's no problem." He had suspected more. "What you got on your mind?"

"I'll explain after you make the call."

Dave Brinkle made the call, and then warned. "You don't need a high school teacher, you need that professional fire fighter."

"I can handle it, Dave. Don't worry."

There was fire in the sheriff's eyes. "I just figured it out." He pointed at him. "You are going to try it yourself, aren't you?"

"Yes sir."

"You don't know a damn thing about putting out these kind of fires."

"Just what I've read."

"It's suicide. I won't let you do it."

There was that look in the youth's eyes again. "Know where I could get some dynamite and a wagon and a team of mules?" Eddy asked.

Sheriff Brinkle realized that no doubt he would be in for a lot more brown nosing. The county would have dynamite, and a team of mules he vaguely remembered seeing somewhere in the area while electioneering. A black man down on the river was still raising vegetables with a team.

Above the roar of the flames, a screaming silver Lear jet approached from the southeast. It swooped in low and passed directly overhead. It then skimmed the desert, gaining altitude, banked to the left, and circled back around the fire. The pilot held the turn tight in order for the oilman, who sat across from him, to get a better view below.

Thomas Drake had received the airborne call only two

hours earlier from his San Sonora office. He had originally been enroute to Louisiana to check progress on his newly acquired offshore oil rig, but landed in Lubbock to pick Gloria up. From there, their destination was Corpus Christi. Gloria would visit her husband Jimmy who was undergoing the Navy pilot training program there. However, less than a hundred miles out of Corpus, he had received the call and directed the pilot to turn back to San Sonora. Gloria was still pissed and pouting. No more so than himself. He had sat around with his finger up his butt and let a peon half-breed, who he had once been a low level employee, discover one of the major lignite beds in the whole southwest. Gloria had asked that he hire him at the ski lodge and now she could damn well repay him. She could help him acquire all or at least part of the youth's holdings. He was mad at himself. He realized that the Majors had been investing heavily in coal property. But they would invest in anything for tax purposes, even solar collectors. But hell, he was an oilman. These damn planes and cars won't run on coal. But coal, it sure as hell would power generating plants that could produce electricity. And those Arabs were giving us a royal screwing on imports.

Coal had been obsolete in the southwest for years, but with dwindling oil and gas reserves, coal fired generating sounded like an attractive consideration to Thomas Drake. "Lignite. Right under my friggin nose."

The plane bounced down on the San Sonora airport runway, devouring almost all its length in stopping and moved slowly back toward the private Drake Oil hanger.

Parnell Green was a small man. Middle aged. His eyes squinted from behind thicker glasses than Eddy remembered from school. But the capabilities of his brain more than offset the deficiency of his impaired eye-sight. He was intelligent. A bachelor. He loved teaching and was still interested in younger women.

When Eddy had suggested that he concoct up enough nitro to blow the fire, he had been reluctant to do so. In fact, so reluctant that Eddy had to remind him of that day in the truck with that senior girl. The teacher consented, and felt sure that Eddy would return the favor someday as he had promised. He would return the next morning, boil it at the house, put it into fruit jars and refrigerate it. But it would be Eddy's responsibility to get it to the fire.

The teacher and Sheriff Brinkle were just leaving when Gloria Drake arrived.

She felt like a horse's ass, being used by her father like this. And she did not like to be used by anyone, including him. Undoubtedly, he was the only living mortal who could do so. And on top of that, she was married and pregnant. She had seen the greed in her father's eyes when he had asked her to come. She supposed she owed him that. But what if Jimmy knew? What would he think if he knew she was being used as bait to lure another fish into her father's financial net? However, she would do this last thing for him and then go to Jimmy. At least she would break clean with Eddy. She would tell him the truth.

Eddy was sitting on the edge of the front porch, staring at the fire, and thinking of Sonya. His thoughts were so engrossed in his feelings and his hatred for the fire, that he did not notice the convertible stopping. Gloria Drake Muhler stepped out of the car, and stared at him. He looked at her as if he was stoned. She relished that idea herself, but realized she now had the baby to think about. She walked over to him and looked down. When his eyes met hers, she could see they were puffed and bloodshot.

"Oh Gloria," he muttered. "I need you so." He pulled her to him and buried his face in her dress.

She did not resist, knowing well that she should, but she had never really felt this much sorrow in her life. She caressed his neck. "What's the trouble, Eddy?"

"That fire killed my sister."

She had heard from her father that an Indian girl was killed in the fire, but she had known Eddy since high school, and didn't realize he had a sister.

"Now, I've got to kill it."

She pushed away. "Maybe my father can help." They

shouldn't be touching like that. "You knew I got married?"

"I read it in the paper."

"I'm pregnant. Can you tell?" She put his hands on her stomach.

"I'm glad you decided to have the baby, Gloria."

Her being there made him feel better. The fire seemed of less importance now. "What you doing out here, Gloria? You didn't come out here just to see the fire."

"Daddy sent me. He wanted me to ask you to come to our house for dinner."

Eddy was suspicious. "Why?"

"He probably wants to try and screw you out of your place somehow."

"I won't let him."

"I don't blame you." She touched his arm. "Really Eddy, he might be of some help with that fire. He's been around the oil fields a long time. He knows a lot about gas fires."

Eddy thought about it. "I had to sell my car, Gloria. I'd be ashamed to park my old pickup in front of a house as nice as yours. Besides, it's not even here now. Butch and Sundance have disappeared in it."

"I'll drive you in." She smiled.

"I've got to have a bath."

"Junior and I will sit on the porch and wait for you."

"If you would like to come in, I'll turn the air on."

"This is fine."

Eddy wondered where Butch and Sundance were. Maybe checking their crop of marijuana, he thought.

The palatial Drake mansion was ultra modern. Geometric in design. Sparkling white stucco, roofed in rustic cedar shakes. The estate was nestled along with other rich Anglo residents in a hilly area on the outskirts of San Sonora.

Eddy felt out of place. Insecure.

They had parked in the garage and walked directly to the kitchen.

It smelled of frying fish. Eddy hated fish, and to him a house this expensive and elaborate shouldn't smell anyway. Mrs.

Drake was busy at the stove. She looked disgusted and weary. She did not speak.

Gloria led him by her, directly to the den where Thomas Drake got up from a massive sofa.

"Nice to see you, Eddy." He paused. "You growing up, boy."

Eddy shook his hand.

"Lydia, the cook got sick and had to go home. See if you can help your mother finish the fish."

Gloria went back toward the kitchen.

"Sit down, Eddy."

Thomas Drake himself felt uncomfortable talking to an ex-employee who might some day be his financial equal. True, he owned much more than the youth. A quarter of the San Sonora field, the gas refinery, the Lear, the lodge and hotel, the yacht, plus the drilling rigs and the house. But many of these things he still owed for. If he sold out today, he would be lucky to break with a clear million. But this turd-head kid. This damn brown skinned kid sitting beside him had discovered a lignite vein as rich as barnyard fertilizer two feet up a bull's behind, right here almost in his back yard. "I understand you discovered a hell of a bed of coal out there on that place of yours, son."

Where did he get that bull? Eddy was impressed with the huge den. He liked it.

"It's pretty good in places. Not so good in others. Average close to eighty feet, I guess."

That elevator to the second floor amused him, as well as reminded him of the time that Drake's Hotel manager wouldn't let him and his momma ride the hotel elevator. Thomas Drake himself had witnessed the incident that day, but paid no attention and probably forgotten it. But he damn sure hadn't. However, now he had the bastard over a barrel. He wanted to see him squirm, even crawl a little maybe. Some day, when he got a little money in his pockets, he would refresh his memory about the elevator incident.

"How much land you got out there?" the oilman asked.

"I'm not really sure. Me and Les Smith are going to have to

get together and figure that out pretty soon. About six sections, could be a couple more."

The millionaire's head worked like a computer. Four or five thousand acres. And to think he had sat around with his finger up his... It was unbelievable. "I flew over this afternoon. See you got yourself a decent gas fire."

"Yes sir. I hoped you might help me with that, sir."

"Cost you a fortune to get Red up here to put it out."

"I know."

The oilman flipped open his coat and removed a contract. He had his lawyer working on it before the jet was halfway back across Texas. Also, his geologist had been busy assessing lignite quantities, and his accountant had been on the phone checking current market demands and valuations and shipping rates. The discovery had been a well kept secret. They had calculated a huge profit could be realized from one half interest in the lignite discovery. Thomas Drake would offer, and no doubt buy half interest in Eddy's property for a half million. That dark half-breed kid would be so flabbergasted at the half million offer, he wouldn't dare turn him down. And he could sit on his ass and make a cool couple million just using his brains. "I'll give you five hundred thousand." He paused. "That's half a million dollars for half interest in that place of yours. Your problems will be over. I'll take care of the fire, and you will be rich."

The figure was impressive, but Eddy remembered what Gloria had said. "I appreciate your offer, Mister Drake, but I'm really not interested in selling."

"Final offer, Eddy." He popped the contract across his hand. "Half a million for half interest. Or I'll give you a mil for it all." He paused, "tell you what let's make it a million for half."

Eddy shook his head and said. "No, sir." He knew he needed the oilman desperately, his money and his experience. He just wasn't positive he would make a good partner. "But I could sure use your help with that fire."

The oilman got up. His brow sweating. "Just sign the damn paper. I'll take care of the fire."

Eddy got up also. "I need your help, Mister Drake. I'll beg

for it if necessary, but I won't sign those papers."

Thomas Drake was livid. He glanced at the youth and sneered. "Take your fire and cram it!" He stormed to the kitchen, demanded that Gloria get him out of his sight. Out of his house.

Gloria smiled within, and Eddy was thankful he would not have to eat those stinking damn fish.

14

The sheriff had delivered the dynamite the previous night while Eddy had been away. He found Sundance and Butch both passed out, probably due to the effects of a combination of drugs and alcohol. He threatened not to leave the stuff and relished the idea of calling off the whole thing. He realized his job was at stake and he had been walking on thin ice ever since Eddy had returned. But this kid had a mystic hold on him that he absolutely positively could not understand. Against his better judgment, he had left it. And this morning as he returned to the ranch house and saw it was still standing, he felt good knowing those crazy assed hippies had not blown it up.

Before going to bed the previous night, Eddy had written out a will. Three-fourths his holdings to the sheriff, the rest divided between Butch and Sundance. He had not slept well. Between that bitch Peaches, the fire, the loss of Sonya, and his visit to the Drake mansion, his mind and body was a boiling cauldron. And the fact of knowing who his real dad was didn't seem to help. He knew what his grandpappy would be doing in a situation like this. He would be in his bedroom on his knees. But Eddy was concerned that he had been doing so much sinning lately his words might not be heard. One thing he did know for sure, just cause you ask for something, didn't mean you were going to get it. And he also realized everything would be done His way, not yours. That made him feel more comfortable, but didn't keep him from feeling jittery as the sheriff pulled up in the front yard.

"I feel purty dang stupid boy," Dave Brinkle said, getting out of the car. "Asking people around town where I could find a wagon and team. After all, that mode of transportation has been obsolete around here for years."

"Did you find one?" Eddy asked.

"Yeah, I found one."

"Great."

The sheriff pushed his hat back. "A black man, truck farming down on the river just out of town. Had a wagon and a pair of old long eared jackasses. Said he would drive em out here today and let you use em for thirty bucks."

"Did he say what they were worth in case I have to buy em?"

"You not figuring on blowing em up, are you?"

"Naw, not if they will walk slow and easy."

"Maybe we better call this thing off, Eddy. Not too late to call that man from Houston. Maybe you could work out a deal with him."

"The man you got coming works for thirty dollars a day. I can afford him."

What the hell, the sheriff thought, it just might work. "Ginny would clean my plow if she thought I would let you do something this dumb."

"Too late to back out now. Mister Green is about finished with the stuff."

Dave leaned against the fender of his wife's Ford station wagon. He could feel the heat through his pants. "Nitro don't like hot weather, Eddy."

You won't be able to drive it up there across that rough terrain."

"That's what the wagon is for." He walked to the car. You get me that rope?"

"In the back seat. Don't forget it's on my bill."

"Don't worry, pay you back when the fire is out."

"Just kidding."

Eddy stepped to the back of the station wagon, opened the door and dragged the rope onto the ground. "I'm going to lead that team right down to the fire. Mister Green thinks I'll be okay at one hundred feet. Probably would survive at fifty."

Dave interrupted. "Keep it a hundred." Paused. "Then what?"

"I'll load it on the truck, aim it at the fire, and turn it loose."

"Sounds like a crazy idea to me." The lawman's mouth was dry. He unwrapped a piece of gum and popped it in his mouth. "Between here and there you just be sure to keep your butt on the end of that rope."

"Don't worry. I will be careful." He looked at Dave and could see the tension on his face. "If things don't feel right I will sell to Thomas Drake. He's offered me a piss pot full of money for half the place and he will take care of the fire."

"Sounds like a damn good idea to me." He looked down the road. "Here comes your wagon and mules."

"I sure do appreciate what you done for me, Dave, but don't you think you better get back to town and pass out a few speeding tickets?"

"Ain't no need to try and get rid of me. I'm on vacation."

Eddy was, and had always been, deeply appreciative of the lawman's help. "I know you been putting your job on the line for me ever since I been back. And for taking care of me after I lost Mom." Tears were forming in his eyes as he moved toward the sheriff. He hugged him. It felt real good. "I want you to know how grateful I am to you and Ginny for all you've done for me. I love you man," and then backed off.

"You got big balls son. Most boys your age still hanging onto their father's checkbook and their mother's dress tail. You've had it rough. I would like to see you get the break in life that you deserve. Even if it does cost me my job."

Eddy picked up the coil of rope and threw it over his shoulder, "I'll pay you back someday."

Arrival of the wagon coincided with the completion of the nitroglycerin.

Parnell Green stepped onto the front porch and said, "It's all yours now. It's in the fridge." He looked at Eddy. "You realize how dangerous the stuff is?"

"Yes sir."

"I take it you're going to transport it in that wagon." He pointed.

"Yes sir."

"It's critical to heat, and sudden jolts. Throw a soft mattress under it and some quilts on top. I think it will be all right." He looked at Eddy. "Just take your time getting there."

"Thanks," Eddy replied gratefully.

"Good luck." Without further conversation the teacher headed for his car.

"I won't forget." Words said but not heard.

The silence was shattered by the screeching of the wagon wheels, rattling of the trace chains, and the clomping of eight big feet.

And above these unusual noises Eddy could hear the Negro driver singing a cheerful spiritual. Eddy needed that.

Butch and Sundance had delivered the old pickup to the rig and were walking back. They got in the back of the wagon before it reached the house and Sundance joined in.

Damn, he didn't know he could sing. It was beginning to sound like one of Grandpappy Gavolin's preaching services, Eddy thought. And if he knew that song, he would join em. He looked at the sheriff. "He sure sounds happy."

"He's happy all right." Dave had been worried and silent. "Should see that old house he's living in, but he don't worry bout things like that. Told me, his mother and daddy were slaves, but were released before they came to New Mexico. Said they settled here on the river and had been truck farming ever since." He motioned for him to circle the wagon near the front porch. "He lost his wife several years ago, but got a daughter living somewhere in California."

Eddy watched as the Negro man slowly turned the mules toward them.

"Wooh dere! Whooo you old mules." He pulled them to a stop.

"You made good time getting them old mules out here, Mose."

"Ya Suh Mister Sheriff, I made purty good time. Des hyen old mules will git yuh dere ifin you got da time." The old grey haired black man tied the reins off and stepped to the ground.

The lawman looked over. "Want to call it off?"

Eddy shook his head. It would be a slow job getting the containers to the rig. He had originally planned two trips just in case. Each trip would probably take over an hour. He would have to maneuver down that makeshift road they had bulldozed in order to get the rig that far out on No Man's Land. It had now been traveled by the fire truck, the sheriff's cruiser and many times in his own pickup. That didn't keep it from being rough.

The sun was almost above them now, it's intensity and brilliance reflecting off aluminum beer cans strewn along the county road. No wind blew. Not a leaf moved on the few trees around the house, and the windmill propeller stood dead still. And the heat bearing downward, as well as the long walk from town, had caused the mules to lather where their harness rubbed against their tough hides. Between their hind legs, a white foamy broth.

The sheriff nodded to Eddy. "Mose, this is Eddy Gavolin."

The youth moved to the black man and firmly shook his hand. "Them mules lead okay Mister Mose?"

"Yuh dey sho will. Yuh kin lead dem ole mules o'mine dout no trouble a'tall."

"Good looking mules." Eddy felt compelled to ask, "Guess you plenty fond of them mules?"

"Deys allsright I reckon." He looked at the mules. "Sho nuff like to swap them critters fer a Cub."

"A Cub."

"Yah Suh. A Farmall Cub." He paused. "Truckin width da Cub be hole lot easy on an ole man liken I is."

"What will a Cub cost you, Mose?"

"Found me a good'n. Used a bit. One thousand dollar. Dey throw de implements in wid it. Whuee....whee. One thousand dollar."

"Will you take a thousand dollars for that wagon and mules," Eddy asked.

"Sho nuff will. I's could buy me that Cub."

Eddy reached for his billfold and pulled out the folded and creased one hundred dollar bills that Checan Martin had given him at the Lodge. That was his last money. He would have to talk to Jake Wilson soon as this fire was out. He handed the money to Mose, "Guess you can buy that Cub now."

With a big smile the Black man reached for the money. Sho do prech'ate dat. I's kin git me dat Cub now. Won't haft feed dem old lazy mules no mo cone."

Eddy turned to the sheriff. "Can you take Mose back to town?"

"You not going to get rid of me that easy. I'll call and have somebody pick him up. He turned to Mose, and pointed. "See that big Mesquite over there. Looks like a good shade. You wait over there till my deputy comes to pick you up."

"Yah Suh." He walked to the wagon and removed a wet burlap wrapped water jug. "Lands sakes a'live, sho nuff gittin hot. I's be waitin fer yo deputy under dat shade Mister Sheriff." He headed for the shade, his faded overalls hanging loosely around him.

Butch moved over to Eddy. "Got the road shoveled in best we could. You would need a road grader to get it smoother. Still going to be rough though."

"What I need and what I got is two different things. How about the truck?"

"We've got it aimed and ready."

Eddy had anticipated transferring the nitro to the bumper of the truck. He would fire her up get her to going toward the rig and then bail out. He just hoped they had it lined up good. He turned to Butch, "You and Sundance throw a mattress and some quilts in the back of the wagon." He retrieved the rope and uncoiled it down the road in front of the mules. He then tied the rope securely to the bridle of the biggest mule.

Sheriff Brinkle walked up and said he would hold the team till he could load up.

Eddy didn't figure it would do any good to argue. He entered the house and reappeared with a foam container cradled in his arms. Packed inside were the glass jars containing the nitro. He glided across the porch, down the steps and to the wagon. He placed the container gently on the mattress, and heaped quilts around it. "I'm scared, Eddy. Damn scared," the sheriff said as he passed by. "Stay on out toward the end of that rope."

Eddy did not answer. When he reached the end of the rope, he reached down and picked it up. He said a short prayer and motioned for Dave to move away. He tied a knot in the end of the rope, wiping sweat from his brow.

The sheriff was at a safe distance. Butch and Sundance were on the side of the house sharing a smoke.

Eddy pulled the slack in the rope, felt tension between him and the big mule's bridle. The mule jerked his head back, lowered it and started to move. The other animal followed suit.

The wagon was moving now, slowly out toward the make-shift road. Eddy was delighted his plan was working so successfully, but was concerned about the lack of control at this distance. He was happy, however, that they had been trained to walk at such a slow pace. He could thank Mose for that. He just hoped when they got there, and he hollered "Woah" they would stop.

He was almost halfway there. Time dragged by. It was hot. A cloud was forming in the southeast. Rain perhaps. Probably not. Not much rain fell in these parts. God, how he loved New Mexico. Almost as much as he loved Gloria. He wished she could be at the fire waiting on him. He would demonstrate his bravery as he jumped from the truck. She could be on the ground waiting for him. They could embrace as the explosion occurred.

He was almost there. He could see Butch, Sundance, and the sheriff following at a safe distance. The mules seemed skittish of the fire. They were walking too close together and seemed to be shying away from it. He moved in hoping for better control. Just a few more feet now to the truck. He moved a little closer and took up the slack in the rope.

The fire crackled. The mules bolted and jerked the wagon against the pickup. Then the explosion.

The sudden eruption sent Eddy violently to the ground. He lay there, frightened, sucking in large breaths of air. Above him the sky seemed cloudy. Not a cloud, however, but an assortment of falling debris. Bits of metal, sand, small rocks, splinters of wood, scraps of leather harness, bloody bits of mule flesh and hair. His ears ringing from the deafening explosion. Within his stomach, a sickening convulsion.

His eyes cleared. He could see the fire still burning. His hopes and pride devastated. His prayers unanswered.

He felt relieved that Gloria had not witnessed his failed attempt. But he would now have to go back to her daddy. He would dread that.

He got to his knees. The blaze was much weaker now. There was a sudden sucking sound as oxygen rushed into the hole seeking to fuel the methane gas again. And then, silence. The pocket of gas had burned itself out. Unbelievable. He figured Grandpappy Gavolin sure must have some pull up-there.

Sheriff Brinkle led the pack as they ran down the road. Sundance was close but Butch had slowed to a fast walk. Too much stress around here. He was about ready to return to the Half-way House.

The sheriff slid down beside Eddy and put his arm around him. After catching his breath he gasped, "You okay, Eddy?"

He wiped his parched lips, and spit sand and saliva on the ground. "Yeah, I'm all right."

Butch shouted from down the road, "Is he okay man?"

Sundance nodded that he was, while wondering how the hell he got the truck, and the fire, both in one shot.

 **15**

The desert between the Flying S and the sheep ranch was dark now. The body of Sonya Silvercloud had been cremated in the fire and hopefully her spirit and soul had reached heaven. Dan Silvercloud realized his daughter had a kind heart. He also felt comfort in the fact that she had made great strides in the right direction while at Brother Rob's Rehab. But she had not been able to make that one big leap to completely conquer her chemical dependency. He himself felt tremendous guilt, that possibly it could be his own past sins that kept her from succeeding. Somehow she had found out. Evidently she had not made it known, but he would do so, at the memorial services in the morning.

It was past midnight. Les Smith was snoring. Peaches was awake, in a drunken stupor, sitting half naked on a bar stool and giggling at the mirror. She dreaded going to bed. She dreaded it, but sleeping with him was one of his many stipulations. If she woke him when she slid in the bed, he would want to feel of her. If she could slip in without waking him, she would have to listen to his snoring or the venting of Pooch's beans. Neither was appealing, but one more stiff drink possibly might make it endurable.

Dan Silvercloud had not been able to sleep. He rocked gently in a rocking chair on the front porch. Gazing toward the big ranch house, his mind churning, he saw the light go out. He had not wanted to disturb his wife and Damond going to the bathroom so he eased around to the side yard to relieve himself. He noticed a light still on at his mother's house. His grandmother would still be watching TV. His mother would probably be dozing in her chair.

Before dark he had saddled his horse, grabbed a shovel from the barn and headed toward the Mexican's gravesite. It had been hard to find. Mesquites had regrown and little evidence existed of any past fence building attempts. Dan suspected that his employer's honesty was questionable when his last attempt at fence building was much closer to Gavolin property. However, the old rancher had hired a survey crew to come out and stake out the fence line. Anyway he looked at it, his ass was in the middle. His boss had ordered him to get the fence built, and his son had torn it down. And if this paper he was in the process of digging up proved that the kid owned this No Man's Land, all hell would break loose.

He walked to his mother's small house, stepped up on her porch and hollered.

"Come on in son," was the reply.

He could hear the sound of whooping Indians, endless gunfire, and the thundering of horses hooves. A single bulb cast shadows down from the ceiling as a small black and white TV bounced sound and eerie reflections off the wall. The old Indian woman sat awake, watching, hoping for, even praying that someday the Indians would end up victorious. But always, it was the white man who won at the end. The battle raged on, Maybe tonight, just maybe.

Dan Silvercloud's heart was deeply burdened as he removed the yellowish worn folded document from his pocket. Surprisingly, it was in decent shape considering the rugged two years in Vietnam and the fruit jar burial it had endured the past twenty years. That had been one tough condom. Perhaps he should have had it on the night the youth was conceived. And he would have if it had been in his possession at that particular time. Unfortunately he had left it hidden in the old trunk he was now looking at, and about to prop his worn boots on. Now if not for this one major problem, he would be content, as his father and uncle before him, to work the rest of his lifetime as foreman on the Flying S.

After the big Indian had dug it up, gently removed, and carefully unfolded it, in his mind there was no doubt, it had been a deed to Gavolin property. It had been beautifully handwritten in ink. Recorded in 1890. Known by all these men present. Declaring Beauford Gavolin the owner of property 16 miles southwest of the town known as San Sonora, New Mexico. The property lay between land homesteaded by E. Gavolin and land owned by the bank. It was divided by the county road on the north and the railroad on the south. Dan remembered conversation when he was a kid that Les and Dora Smith had bought the huge ranch from the local bank.

He got up and walked over and turned the TV down. He looked at his grandmother. She was getting old. Her dark skin was wrinkled. She wouldn't wear her false teeth and her chin jutted out. And he could see she was annoyed because he had turned her sound down. He turned to his mother who, it turns out, was still awake. "Mama, I need to talk to you."

She motioned to the old tattered couch. "Sit."

He wondered why she didn't buy new furniture. She should spend some of the money Mrs. Smith had left her. Miss Dora had been very thoughtful in leaving the Silvercloud women money as a reward for their ability to provide for her needs in her later years. His wife was spending hers on Damond's college education, but his mother and his aunt were just sitting on theirs.

"Well, what you want? Something sure must be eatin on you."

His long kept secret was about to be exposed. "The half-blood," he gazed into her eyes. "The boy that belonged to the sheep-woman." He hesitated. "He belongs to me. You got a grandson Mama."

She spat a stream of snuff juice in a coffee can and looked up. "He killed Sonya."

"He didn't kill her, Mama."

"His contraption did."

126

He couldn't dispute that. "It was the will of the gods, Mama."

"You've brought shame upon the family, Dan."

The tall Indian felt uncomfortable. "I am ashamed of myself, Mama, but I sure need your advice." He held up the deed. "You remember this piece of paper you didn't burn years ago. You told me to hang on to it. I think it's a deed showing Eddy owns the property between here and the sheep ranch."

She had anticipated this situation and knew exactly what her son would do. She also knew what Les Smith would do when he found out that she had not burned the document. He would kick the whole damn family off the ranch.

She got out of her chair and headed for the TV. She looked over at Dan. "You just do the right thing, son. We will be just fine." She turned the sound back up. "Don't forget to pick me up in the morning. I want to get a good look at that grandson of mine."

This morning, at the rig where she had perished, there would be a memorial for Sonya Silvercloud. The service would be conducted by a chaplain who had befriended Dan Silvercloud before his discharge from the Marine Corp. Other than Butch, Sundance, and Jake Wilson, there was no one other than her family in attendance. There would be no church for the services. No flowers for the coffin. No coffin for the grave. No grave for the internment. Her body had been cremated in the fire and her soul ascended higher than the smoke into the heavens above.

The chaplain, surrounded by saddened family and friends. Two slightly different races, void of prejudice, both with burdened hearts. Eddy Gavolin divided. His body and soul, half Indian, half Anglo. His eyes moist.

"And now, may the deceased, Sonya Silvercloud, rest in peace and in heaven. Amen."

Dan Silvercloud walked over to Eddy and embraced him. He handed him the folded worn and stained piece of paper which he had protected for all these years. "This might really be important to you. I think it might be the deed your family has been looking for." Not wanting to look Eddy in the eye, he looked at the ground. "I didn't tell her but somehow she knew." He paused and looked up, "Somehow she knew she was your sister."

The Indian slid on his hat, and walked off.
The youth stood tall, bewildered.
The Silvercloud women eyeballed him real good.

76

Forty miles out of Artesia, Les Smith sat hunched over, sitting on the top railing of the Double B Ranch corral fence. His old rump, tough as cowhide, being exposed for years to these exact same circumstances. He watched from beneath the shade of his wide brim Stetson as the cowboys made preparations to try and cut the big Brahma bull out of a large herd of Double B livestock. His thoughts were meandering. He remembered back to the early thirties. He was then just a stapling youth of 24 or 25. He wasn't quite sure which. The Depression was still in progress. Times were hard for the sheep men then. Damn hard. Then came the drought, it didn't rain for more than a year. The sparse grass was dying. Sheep were dying. Just as well, though, as they weren't worth anything. The land, thousands and thousands of acres selling for a dollar an acre. Still one of the sheep men tried to tough it out. He was Beauford Gavolin. Tough and rugged. It was said then, Les Smith remembered, that the sheep rancher, when a young man won the fight with the devil, started preaching, and stayed on the land.

He realized that he himself could not have stayed if it had not been for his wife's family money. She had been a few years older than him but her daddy's money had more than compensated for the age difference. Her family didn't care for him much, and was hell bent he would never get his hands on any part of the Cain ranch. That property had been earmarked for the Cain brothers, the oldest would inherit the Palace. Usually the daughter was rewarded with the home place. This situation was different.

However, the old man did take care of his daughter financially. He purchased nearly fifty thousand acres of New Mexico range land for her and bought her the finest multi-story house Sears Roebuck had to offer.

Les had wanted the house built back further onto the property to get away from the sheepman. Miss Dora wanted it built down on the county road where the people of San Sonora could drive out on Sunday afternoon and covet her good fortune. Unfortunately, to get close to the road they put the house too close to Gavolin property for his comfort. He immediately researched the land situation and to his good fortune discovered the desolate property between him and the sheep ranch was a different parcel from the main operation. With a loan from his wife's daddy, he would buy it. But.

The Cain Ranch was located in the panhandle of West Texas. It would have qualified as one of the larger ranches in the state, but half of it was in Oklahoma. And old man Cain had anticipated that when the boys graduated from college, and returned to the ranch, they would contribute an even greater dynasty to the Cain name. That's not exactly the way things had worked out as they returned, one by one. They returned with their wild ways, wild women, and fast cars. They feuded among themselves and squandered most of the remainder of the family money.

When the old man died, they divided the ranch and two of the sons sold their part immediately. Tom, the oldest, had decided to change his ways somewhat, go to work, and hang on to his part of the ranch. However, he was the first family member to die and left his part to his older sister, Mrs. Dora Smith. Unfortunately, she had died shortly thereafter and Les still retained ownership of that property. Her other two younger brothers constantly hounded him to return it to them. He really didn't need it but refused to give it back to them because they were too sorry. That's the reason Miss Dora had left her half of the Flying S to the First Baptist.

Fortunately for him, she had left him a lifetime estate. If she hadn't, some of them damn money hungry Baptists would have already sold it by now. And probably, with his luck, to a large hog raising corporation. He sure couldn't think of anything worse that could happen to him than having sheep crap on one side of him and hog crap on the other. Unless of course it would be, having to look out his upstairs window every morning at a big black hole in the bowels of Mother Earth and watching dirt moving equipment moving around in it like piss ants around a doughnut hole. Oil was just as bad. At least Thomas Drake, over in the north part of the county, was sucking it out with a big straw. To Les that sure as hell would be better than tearing into, and clawing and gnawing at her innards.

The half-breed was pushing him. He was ready to let off some steam. He would do it now. The Double B cowboys had just run that bad ass bull into the loading corral. That big sucker had already killed one rodeo cowboy. And that cowboy was the son of a good friend of his.

Amidst the whooping and the hollering of several of the Double B cowboys, the big Brahma charged into the corral, anxious to maim or mutilate anything or anyone that opposed him. Large, powerful, gray and graceful. His pointed horns curved high above his shaking head, a strong neck forward of a massive hump and slim hips. The bull stopped and stared at Les Smith. A killer instinct visible in his glassy eyes. He pawed the ground daring him to climb down from his perch on the fence into the corral.

Brad Hemphill, the owner of the ranch, popped up beside Les Smith. He was perspiring heavily. "That's a mean sonofabitch there. No good for my rodeo stock any more. Be glad to be rid of em. What you want a killer like that for, Les?"

Les Smith slid his billfold from his back pocket. He removed a thousand dollars and handed it to the other rancher. Then eased off the fence and walked to his pickup. When he returned, he stood the 30-30 carbine against the corral fence. Slowly he slipped a pair of soft leather gloves onto his calloused hands.

"What you aimin to do, Les?"

"What does it look like?"

"Looks a mite like you gonna shoot em."

"He's my bull, ain't he?"

"He's yore bull."

His gloves on now, Les Smith climbed back atop the fence. The bull had not moved. He positioned himself, took careful aim, and in rapid succession, pumped three shots into the bull's head. The bull fell. Les Smith waited a few seconds before saying, "You boys can eat him or you can call the soap wagon. He'll be worth a few bucks fer soap."

Hemphill muttered under his breath, unbelieving, "He shore must be pissed at somebody."

Les turned to him and spoke almost nonchalantly, "Brad, you said earlier you wanted to sell them buffalo of yorn."

"Sho would."

"Magnificent animals, them buffalo."

"Yep."

"Have your men round em up." He laid the rifle across his legs and removed his gloves. "I'll be back Monday to pick em up."

It would be a lonely ride home by himself. He could have brought one of the cowboys, but they would not have talked. He could have brought Hooch or Pooch and they would not have stopped talking. And now that Miss Dora had passed, they were becoming more independent. Course, that was because she had left each one of them a piss pot full of money.

He had fallen heir to Hooch and Pooch when he moved to New Mexico. Old man Cain had sent his best cowboy and his best chuck wagon cook to take care of his only daughter. At first Les had considered them spies but later realized they had been instrumental helping him make the Flying S a thriving cattle operation. Hooch headed up the ranch and Pooch handled things around the house.

In return for their hard work, Les had built them a comfortable bunkhouse. The cowboys had bunks in the big room but they each had private quarters. Les had offered to install indoor plumbing for them but they wanted no part of that. They preferred a two hole outhouse out back and positively nobody else was allowed to use it. And Pooch's kitchen was also outside. A lean-to on the side of the bunkhouse. It contained a monster grill and three Dutch ovens. In the winter a large stack of mesquite on the north side broke the bitterness of the harsh wind. Smoke continually seeped from the roof chimneys and the smell of food was usually in the air.

Pooch didn't do any cooking in the Big House. He had made that plain to Miss Dora. He did his cooking in the shed. That was fine with her. She would just send her kitchen cook out to fetch it in for her and Les. He would teach the cooks to fix special items he knew Miss Dora really liked. She loved chocolate gravy. Steaks and brisket were his specialty, but he could do wonders with a Dutch oven. He could make vegetables taste like ice cream and fruit cobblers taste better than lipstick to a sex starved man. And his biscuits were out of this world. They would melt in your mouth, if you had homemade butter to go with them. And for the hell of it, he had been known to purposely forget to put butter on his grocery list. To get it, Hooch would have to rope a cow, tie her legs and try and keep her still while one of the cowboys milked her. After all he was the main cowboy. Later they would churn up some fresh butter.

Pooch claimed Hooch didn't do anything. Sat on his butt all day riding around the ranch giving orders. Hooch claimed Pooch didn't do anything. He would get the meat on them glowing coals, and the beans boiling. Then sit his skinny butt in a big rocker till eating time, chawing and spittin tobacco juice. And when it came to giving orders, Pooch was plenty good. The cowboys knew who was spooning out the food, and the higher you jumped when Pooch hollered, the higher he heaped the spoon when you came through the food line. And he didn't wash any dishes. You washed your own plate, fork and cup. But at least you didn't have to clean them in the sand like out at the old Cain chuck wagon. The shed had running water.

What really ticked Hooch off was when Pooch would sit on his hole, and spit down the other. Course the other hole was his, and it didn't bother Pooch a bit to get some of that brown juice on his seat. Looked like crap. He was about ready to change his mind and let Les build him one of them indoor flushers.

Les Smith realized things were changing. Hooch and Pooch were older now and sure seemed different since Miss Dora had passed on and stuffed their saddlebags full of money. Or possibly the reason was, their resentment of him marrying Peaches. Possibly it was because they were jealous of him. He was sure they would like to have a wife, but realized they were too stubborn and too contrary to find a woman who would put up with them. And it didn't hurt to have plenty of money. He was spending a small fortune on Peaches. But what to hell, he didn't have anybody else to leave it to anyway. As long as she made him happy.

Peaches had been acting weird lately. He couldn't figure out why. She realized he was a horny old bastard when she said, "I do." And the dancing, he paid her better than her previous employer and he figured the benefits were much better. And if she just could make him happy till he died, she would be on easy street. And if she didn't, there most likely would be an annulment. And that embarrassing fling she had with the car salesman pushed him to his limit. After she sobered up she promised nothing like that would happen again, and she would get naked and jump in bed anytime he desired. But she sure seemed miserable and not the least bit interested now. Making love to her was like lying on top of a warm watermelon. He had ordered five hundred and fifty dollars worth of Brother Rob's Chakras jewelry for her to wear. The brochure advertised the seven colors of the rainbow and had mystical powers. A different color for each part of the body. He had ordered her ear rings, a necklace and a bracelet with orange settings. Orange was the color for the pelvic area. She had worn it often but it had failed to stimulate her sexual organs. Maybe he should have ordered brown. That was the color for the brain. However, he reckoned he was a little bit fortunate. That twenty dollar brass bracelet he had ordered for himself from Brother Rob sure had seemed to help his old rumatiz.

His biggest problem now was trying to eat that gourmet

cooking them two chefs of Peaches' served up every day. That just wasn't enough for a working man to live on. He usually would go to the shed afterward for a bowl of Pooch's beans or chili, a slice of brisket or a steak. And definitely, plain old biscuit, steak and eggs was out of the question for breakfast, if it was up to them two chefs of hers. You would be lucky if you got three grapes, a piece of toast, and one egg served up all fancy.

77

Gloria Drake miscarried aboard her father's jet on the return trip to Corpus Christi Naval Air Station. She had been alone except for the pilot.

18

Eddy Gavolin had already called Checan Martin in Dallas. She could not come immediately however, because she was involved in a transaction of property proposed for one of the largest shopping centers in the Southwest. She assured him, though, that about one more good tumble with one of the senior members of the prospective buying corporation and she would undoubtedly have the deal sewn up. When this was completed, she would charter a plane for the trip to San Sonora. He wasn't to look for her for about three days. She would call him to meet her. She had seemed extremely glad to hear from him and about his discovery.

Eddy was desperate for money now. He needed a lawyer and a surveyor. For once and for all, he wanted that property line between him and the Flying S Ranch established. But he didn't want to get the Silvercloud family fired until he could take care of them, and no doubt about it, when the old rancher found out that Dan's mother had not burned the deed, all hell would break loose. It could be fruitless to talk to Jake Wilson again. He already owed him for the rig, and even though still standing, it was virtually destroyed. The Sundance Kid suggested that he talk with Brother Rob at the Half Way House.

It was a rather special occasion for the three of them. They had hardly set foot off the sheep ranch in months. In fact, such a special occasion for Butch and Sundance that it prompted them to take a bath.

Brother Rob's Half Way House, Eddy reckoned, was about half way all right. About half way up the mountain. It was an old abandoned lumber camp nestled into the Guadalupe Mountains.

The air conditioner in Sheriff Brinkle's old station wagon had quit functioning soon after leaving the ranch, and they were glad to finally be there, sweaty or not. Up the mountain road, the worn Chevy was averaging only about ten miles to the quart. The pull up the mountain and the heat was causing the transmission fluid to boil out. They'd had to stop often and add a quart from the dwindling case in the rear. It got so aggravating that they had taken turns. Eddy hoped they would be able to coast down, thus avoiding this inconvenience.

The surroundings were serene, even if the setting wasn't. Parked beneath the trees was the damndest array of temporary shelters Eddy had ever witnessed. Old buses, vans, trailers and tents. Few with tires and wheels.

The war in Vietnam had been over for years. Evidently that war had spawned a new revolution, not seen on this earth in modern times. A flood of a new breed of youth protesting authority, living in communes, in cars and buses, on the streets and in the trees. Living and loving freely. Do your own thing, drop out of society, turn on to LSD or other mind altering drugs. Explore your relationship with your consciousness. Release your permissiveness and transcend into an ecstasy of love, beauty, music and fun.

The hippy was easily recognized. Usually sandals or bare feet, men with shaggy long hair and beards. Women braless. Their clothing gleaned from throw-away, flea markets or second hand shops. Usually redesigned by tie-dying or tearing when it came into their possession. Show a little, live a lot.

However, this original group of hippies had dissipated back into the culture to which they had originally been conceived. And the younger replacement generation discovered their predecessors' milder mind altering drugs were insufficient. They pursued harsher, highly addictive drugs such as amphetamines and opiates.

Drug addiction ran rampant across the country and this

area is where Brother Robert "Rob" Newberry chose to create his ministry. Brother Rob was not an ordained minister because he had dropped out of seminary to join a gospel singing group. This was where he first learned of his strong influence on people. His voice was strong, his body young and his face obviously appealed to the opposite gender. And after traveling the country with the group for several months and seeing the need, he felt the time was right. He was ready to preach. And to his good fortune, Sister Rosilee Cashion, a singing sensation, had been one of his earliest converts. She was heir apparent to the Cashion Cosmetic fortune. And her money, if Daddy would turn loose, along with his ambitions, could easily jump-start his ministry. People assumed they were married, but each had their own trailer house and Cadillac.

Brother Rob believed the Bible in its entirety. He loved, felt loved and as David before him, reasoned he would also be forgiven. Admittedly he would probably gaze upon a naked woman on a rooftop, and might even invite her to his bedroom, but would never try and have her husband killed in battle.

Sundance pointed to a sign. "Well, we're here."

Eddy glanced at the sign. SEARCH FOR THE LOST. The steeple stood as high as the pines.

At the rear of the church was a two-story dormitory. DRUG REHABILITATION. A smaller sign beneath. Donated by Cashion Cosmetics.

Sundance guided Eddy around to the side of the church to the office.

Eddy coasted the wagon to a stop. As they were getting out, Sundance pointed to a blinking red light on the office door. "Guess Brother Rob is recording his sermons and singing."

"Come on, Eddy, we will show you around," Butch suggested.

Eddy followed them to the back of the dorm. Several girls were helping prepare the evening meal. They seemed happy to see the pair back.

"How bout something cold to drink?" Sundance asked. "Tea okay."

"Beer be better."

"No beer here, you know that." She handed them all a glass of tea.

They were thirsty and guzzled it down. Afterward they headed for a large metal building that was called The Kings Manufacturing Co. A dozen young men, long haired Anglos, were busy manufacturing Chakras healing jewelry. Silver jewelry embedded with a stone of one of the colors of a rainbow. An ancient cure for your brain on down to your sexual organs.

One of the men yelled as they passed by, "Man, it's good to see you got out of jail." He moved closer. "Bring any of that good grass man?"

"Naw, that redneck sheriff burned it." He looked at Eddy and grinned.

"Man, I'm dying," the worker replied.

They moved on down to a restricted area. Bars were on the windows and a heavy lock on the entry. Only a few of the most trusted rehabs in remission were allowed to work here. This was the anointed cloth factory. Several young women sat around a large table. Some cutting small pieces of material from a large bolt. Others sprinkling it with an oily solution. The material was being packaged and addressed. There was a good reason for this area to be secure. Brother Rob had caught several of the severely addicted sipping the anointing solution. The mixture contained perfume, fish oil and alcohol.

They received a tumultuous welcome when they entered. It was hot inside and the girls were scantily clad.

"Guys, this is Eddy Gavolin," Butch said.

Eddy tipped his hat. A habit he had been taught by Lambert.

That sure impressed the girls.

Butch walked around behind the table, bent down and kissed a buxomly tanned girl on the neck. He looked over at Eddy. "Man, I want to show you the finest pair of tits you've ever seen." He lifted her large breasts out of her halter and exposed them.

Eddy couldn't figure out why, but he tipped his hat again.

Everybody laughed.

Butch and the girl hit the exit ahead of Eddy and Sundance. They headed for a grouping of young pines out back. Evidently, to renew their acquaintance.

Sundance had pointed out the weaving looms. Several girls were busy weaving Navajo replicas. The mail order department was near the rear exit. Stacks of merchandise were packed and ready for shipment to Brother Rob's radio audience.

Eddy followed Sundance back to the studio. The red light was still flashing. He eased the door open and they quietly stepped inside.

There was singing going on and to Eddy's surprise, Sundance ambled over to the microphone and joined in.

To keep offerings active, and to keep the sales of his advertised products flooding from his warehouse, Brother Rob realized his radio ministry must relate to the listener. The singing must be great and the message above average, because there were numerous other preachers out there competing for the same money. His hard work and dedication had been rewarding. His income was now so sufficient that he had started construction on a large lavish house further up the mountain.

The singing of Brother Rob and Sister Rosilee ranked high in listenership and set the perfect stage for his message. He preached a "feel good" message instead of "fire and brimstone." He suggested that men and women should pray for health, happiness and prosperity regularly. And offerings and good works for his church would be received and put to good use as a reprieve to their sins. Often affluent people would be drawn into his airwaves web and large amounts could be extracted from them.

He would record the tapes at the church, then transport them across the border to Old Mexico for broadcasting. Rates were much cheaper there and transmitters did not fall under the rule of the U.S. Federal Communications Commission. In the early evening his program could be blasted across a big part of the United States. His golden voice beckoning, "Cash, checks, or money orders, folks." All the items he sold were profitable.

Loans by mail, the eternal anointed cloth, a miraculous feel good excelsior that gave you vim, vigor, and vitality and a herbal ointment guaranteed to cure anything between a headache and toe itch. This miracle product would supposedly also cure traumatism, rheumatism, hemorrhoids, and impotency. And the Chakras rainbow jewelry. Order a free brochure to see what color stone to wear for your particular afflicted area.

It was Brother Rob's belief that many common body aches could be cured by the power of one's mind. And surprisingly, his message and his products evidently gave his audience that power because he was seldom ever asked for a refund.

But the church itself leaned to a different type congregation than the radio audience. This was his true ministry. Run-a-ways, transients, and addicts. He felt his true calling was drug addiction, and deeply felt the possibility of breaking the habit without divine intervention was an impossibility. He exploited the devil vehemently for pushing these mystical mind altering drugs upon his young congregation. He promised if they would only commit, the devil would be defeated and their habit could be broken.

Brother Rob removed the tape and shut down the recording console. Then stepped to his private office and motioned Eddy and Sundance inside.

Sister Rosilee was already there. Eddy glanced at her. She was wearing a white robe and he was about 99 percent positive she was naked beneath it. She smiled at him and it made him feel jittery.

"Eddy, this is Brother Robert."

Eddy shifted his hat and shook his hand.

Sundance turned. "And this is my little sister, Rosilee."

Her hand was smooth and soft. It felt so good to Eddy that he could have held it the rest of the day.

Brother Rob slid in behind an enormous desk and sat down. "Sundance said you needed to borrow some money."

"Yes sir."

"Said you needed at least ten thousand."

Eddy was surprised that Sundance had asked for so much.

Brother Rob looked at Eddy. "We don't usually make loans that large."

Sister Rosilee stepped over to the desk. "Make the check for twenty thousand, Rob."

Eddy cringed with disbelief.

Then she turned to Sundance and said, "When are you going to get your act together and go home? Daddy needs you."

Brother Rob didn't argue. He just started writing.

Eddy glanced at Sister Rosilee again. Sure didn't look like she was wearing the pants. And that thin gown sure was turning him on.

19

*P*erhaps it was a minor thing. To Eddy however, it loomed liked a monster tearing into his innards. He felt a seething guilt about destroying old Mose Ripley's team and wagon even though he had bought them, as well as the burdens he had recently placed upon Sheriff Dave Brinkle. He himself should have gone to the black man, explaining, and possibly consoling him, instead of letting Dave Brinkle handle the situation. He should have handled it personally. He had been hiding behind the sheriff's badge since returning to San Sonora. He would be his own man from this day forward he told himself. To hell with the surveyor and the lawyer for now. He would pay his debts to those he owed—old Mose Ripley, Sheriff Dave Brinkle, and Butch and Sundance. These were the people he felt uncomfortably indebted to.

Sheriff Brinkle, he knew, yearned for involvement in politics. He learned of this political desire his senior year while the then Deputy Brinkle was politicking for sheriff. His dream was to be elected sheriff, then county judge, district judge, and possibly someday even state representative. But this could wait till later. It would have to wait till later. Someday though, when he was on his feet, he would help the sheriff, and thus fulfill his debts.

Butch and Sundance. They were crazy asses he knew, but he was deeply indebted to them also. They had stayed at the Half Way House because of his denial to let them bring a couple of girls back to the ranch.

Before leaving, Eddy had offered them some of the money he had gotten from Brother Rob. They had turned him down flat. Money was immaterial to them. Eddy had been persuasive, demanding to repay them in some way. Their desires had been simple. Five acres each near the timber at the back side of the place. It was near the government owned National Forest, and lignite was non-existent. They wanted to build a self sufficient habitat, using the wind, the sun, and the earth to provide their needs. With exception, of course, of their sexual needs. Eddy knew they no doubt would take care of this also. Tomorrow he would go to the local title company and get the paper work started. Later, he hoped to help them financially with their weird project. Today, he would make peace with Mose Ripley.

Unknown to Eddy Gavolin, for years Todd Muhler, Thomas Drake, and Jed Jutman had owned Jutman and Son Realtors. Jed was basically the front man for these two richest men in the county. Real estate was not their forte, but making more money was. They had carefully manipulated the city council. Their purpose, to get city water and sewer nearer to Mose Ripley's truck farm, which was located just on the outskirts of San Sonora. Their efforts had been so successful that now the choice property sat on the boundary of the city limits, and the town's conveniences were easily accessible. The property, in their eyes, was probably the few choice pieces of property available in Southeast New Mexico. It bordered the San Sonora river on the rear and a state highway on the front and was a perfect location for a modern shopping center.

Their plan was almost complete, lacking only the signature of Mose's only daughter. She was due to arrive in San Sonora the following week and the sale could be consummated and they could sit at the bar at the country club bragging of their ingenuity. Buying cheap and selling at a greedy extravagant profit. Actually, they had already made arrangements with a Dallas consortium to sell the property for a large shopping center. Muhler would retain enough of the property for a large office building for rental purposes, as well as housing his aviation headquarters. Drake would build a large modern hotel and move his drilling and productions operations from the old downtown hotel. In anticipation of the move he had already listed his old Drake Hotel with a Dallas company for them to sell.

Eddy slowed the station wagon and coasted past the vegetable stand and turned down the lane to the house. The house was old and weathered but looked comfortable and peaceful. Smaller, but not much different from the old Gavolin ranch house. But unfortunately, Eddy had witnessed little peacefulness in their house since his mom had taken in Lester Snodgrass years before. A brief thought ran through his mind that he might move the old house over on the river when he sold the majority of the ranch to the coal company. Only problem with that, he reckoned he would be neighbors with Butch and Sundance. Fortunately though, it was customary for the mining company to give original owners first chance to buy the land back and Eddy definitely would be buying the ranch back.

The barn was dilapidated and leaning. The rusty torn corrugated roof moved in unison with the swaying of the fruit tree limbs in the orchard. Eddy figured it would not endure another light wind storm and would surely bury the small tractor in the debris. The windmill blade was missing so many fins it had almost ceased turning but that did not matter to Mose. Thanks to Thomas Drake the city had run water to his house.

The soil was rich, and the old Negro for years sustained a living by planting, harvesting and peddling his home grown produce to local housewives. To Eddy, the place looked comfortable but not prosperous. He assumed Mose Ripley's prosperity was his happiness.

Old Mose rocked contentedly in a chair on the sagging front porch. He spat tobacco juice between his fingers as Eddy approached.

"Mister Ripley."

"Dat's me."

"I'm Eddy Gavolin. I came to tell you how sorry I am for destroying the mules."

"Da wuz yore mules. Youze paid fer em." He motioned to Eddy. "Git in outa dis sun, boy."

Eddy stepped onto the porch. The shade felt cool.

"Bought me that Cub." He motioned to a straight chair. "Sit yo self, boy."

Eddy took a seat, nearly falling through the porch. "I just feel terrible about what happened. I want to apologize for what I done."

The old Negro looked at Eddy. "De sheriff, he done tole me bout all dem problems yous has. De po gal whut wuz killed in dat bad ole fire'n'all."

"It's out now, Mister Ripley, thanks to you. Just sorry about your mules."

"Wuz gonna haft to part wid dem ole mules purty soon anyways. Reckon deys jest soon went dat whey as to de soap factor."

"Why is that, Mister Ripley?"

"Sho hates to," he spit again. "I's sellin dis ole place. Jest waiten on muh dauter to git in from California next week. She done wen'n' hitched herself up tos a white man. De Lord onlst nos whut dis ole worl comin to."

Eddy looked around him. He was impressed by the location. San Sonora was growing this way. "Who are you selling to, Mose?"

"Dat mista real estate man and Mista Drake gonna giv us'es a thousan an acre. Neva heare offin no farmin land being wurth dat. Land sakes'o'live, bad is I's wanted to, I's dis cutn't tun dat down."

"How many acres you got here, Mister Ripley?"

Mose was not used to being called mister by whites. He liked the sound. "Near bout eighteen acres."

"You signed papers already?"

"I's waitin on muh litel gal."

Eddy was thinking of the $20,000 check in his billfold. He realized that was the last penny he had to his name. He also realized the old man was going to get a royal screwing. "I'll give twenty thousand Mister Riply."

He sure liked being called mister, even if that boy wasn't quite all the way white. "Dats mo dan da gonna giv me. Reckon I's sel to yous iffin you got da mony."

Eddy had wanted to buy a car, but to hell with that. He reluctantly removed the check from his billfold and handed it to Mose. "Hang on to this Mister Ripley." He shook his hand, "I'll be back in the morning."

prefer that is unreadable since . . . would take years to find
company to get the coal mining and be ready to dig them. And
the electricity they could start digging on the slack return
own at the most every time had fixed a serving fee. . . .

20

*C*hecan Martin had just completed perhaps her final sex enhanced real estate transaction. The deal was finalized in a king sized bed, in a luxurious room, high above the streets, in a downtown Dallas hotel. When Eddy had notified her that he had located deep veins of coal on the sheep ranch, she immediately dispatched her assistant to San Sonora to locate adjoining landholders that might be willing to sell their land. And she had hit a jackpot. She had just purchased fourteen sections of land across the tracks from Eddy's property. This deal could easily propel her to the top rungs of the elite Dallas real estate ladder. Or possibly retirement. It was a simple transaction.

She had bought the place from a Jewish man who, when younger, envisioned a ranch there. But as the years passed, he became less interested and seemed content splitting his time between his North Dallas mansion and his Mexican villa. But even though he had plenty of money, he would have undoubtedly been less prone to sell if he had known about the vein of lignite across the tracks. Her profits, if deep veins of coals were prevalent on the majority of the property, would be sizeable.

Fortunately for Checan, Eddy had contacted her and advised that he had received the original deed for the disputed property between the sheep ranch and the Flying S. Also that he had signed a contract to buy half the large ranch from the Baptist church. He explained to her he could not take control till the old rancher died. She could not believe his good fortunes and did not foresee that as a problem since it would take years for the coal company to get the cogs turning and be ready to dig there. And in the meantime they could start digging on the sheep ranch as well as the property she had just taken a screwing for.

27

*E*ddy had a hangover and nearly overslept.

He whipped by the mini mart for a coke and apple pie. The pie tasted old. He spent his last six dollars on gas and agonized over the thought of having to ask Jake Wilson for a loan. He had borrowed twenty thousand dollars from him to buy the rig, and even though still standing, the fire had destroyed its value. He had borrowed twenty thousand from Brother Rob and Sister Rosilee and spent it the next day on a truck farm and roadside vegetable stand. He somehow had sure gotten his tail in a crack. Maybe Checan would have some ideas. He was sure looking forward to seeing her but it had chapped his butt because she had decided to stay at the Drake Hotel instead of one of the local motels. He sure as hell had not forgotten the incident he and his mom had encountered with the hotel elevator ride when he was a youngster. That remembrance was still burning within him as she opened the door for him.

At the ski resort Checan Martin had devoured Eddy's virginity and conceded that had been the last time she had reached complete sexual satisfaction. Now she felt weak staring at him in the doorway. He looked so different now, troubled and much older for such a short period of time. She feared those moments of ecstasy she had witnessed at their first meeting would never be re-enacted. But in return for those few moments, and the opportunity afforded her with his discovery of lignite, she would be dedicated to him. She would use her real estate prowess to assist his financial future, as well as her body to fill any needs he might desire.

They did not speak but embraced eagerly. She slammed the door shut, and with animal instincts they grappled each other while struggling toward the bed.

The encounter had been fulfilling for both, but not a passionate act of deep felt love. Now his head was between her breast, weeping. He didn't know if his deep need to cry was his sorrow, his loneliness, or his sanity.

Minutes before he had been her lover. Now she felt love, as if he was her son. What an eerie feeling. Two distinct kinds of love, so different, so real. Certainly she was old enough to be his mother.

When the tears subsided, he looked up and asked, "Why are you staying in this dump?"

She smiled. "It's for sale and since you are going to need a place to stay soon, I thought you might want to buy it."

He pondered his situation. "I sure would like that, but right now I need a car worse than a place to stay."

"Why don't you buy one?"

"Cause my ass is broke. I borrowed twenty thousand dollars yesterday but bought a truck farm out on the highway before I could get it to the bank.

No way did she think it might be possible, but asked anyway. "How big?"

"Eighteen acres. Thomas Drake offered him eighteen thousand and I knew he was cheating the old man, so I offered twenty."

She couldn't believe what she was hearing. Drake was cheating hell out of him all right. "You got a contract?"

"Nope, but he's got my check in his pocket. If you will help me, we will get him signed up today." He paused. "One problem though."

"What's that?"

"His daughter lives in California and we need her signature."

"You mean we're going to have to go to California?"

"She will be coming down here in a day or two."

"We don't need to wait." She visualized the plans for the shopping center she had seen on Jim Langston's desk in Dallas. "Do you think he would be willing to fly?"

"Probably not."

"You better go buy you a new car then."

He looked stunned. "What with?"

She grinned. "Tell them to charge it to the company."

"What company?"

"How about Gavolin and Martin Investments?" She hugged him. "I'll call Dallas and have fifty thousand dollars transferred into your new account." She patted him on the rear end. "If we sneak this deal through, you'll make enough to buy this old hotel if you want it."

His mind was racing. "I want it."

When Eddy left the room he was shaking his head with disbelief and thinking that his old Grandpappy Gavolin, once again, sure must have some pull up there.

While Eddy bought the new vehicle, Checan had transferred money to his account, bought the Drake Hotel for him, dressed, and eaten breakfast. And now, wearing a business suit and carrying a briefcase, she was in her groove. Ready for the rest of the day. They would stop by and discreetly pick up a contract. She would have to word a contract for deed so as not to arouse suspicion of their intentions. If Drake got wind of what they were up to, he would call her cohorts in Dallas and her ass would be up the creek.

Checan appraised property often but was in awe of the surroundings. Rich and lush and green. So different from the miles of desert she had passed through on the drive from El Paso.

Eddy had driven down the street to the river and returned via a white rock road adjacent to Mose Ripley's property line. Eddy parked the new Chevy station wagon at the vegetable stand, and asked. "Well, what do you think?"

"Looks like a damn good place for a shopping center." She flipped open her notepad and started writing. "What did you say his name is?"

"Mose Ripley."

"And the daughter?"

"No idea."

"Let's go ask him."

Eddy had been right. "Naw suh." Old Mose had no intention of flying.

Checan called and made arrangements for them to meet Mose's daughter, Mareena, and her husband at a Phoenix hotel. She then called Chuck in Dallas, asked him to get deed information from Jim, and fly to Arizona and meet them. She was now definitely in her element, but later her tail would be tired and bored on the trip.

22

The tragic news was of little importance nationally, but both major wire services in the Southwest carried the gruesome story. The news was read solemnly by radio and television announcers, while most newspapers throughout the state carried the story, headlined: Wife of prominent San Sonora Rancher trampled to death by buffalo in one of state's most freakish accidents.

A column in the obituary section of *The San Sonora Daily News* read:

> Funeral services will be held at 2:30 P.M. for
> Mrs. Nancy "Peaches" Smith, wife of local rancher,
> Les Smith. She was killed late Monday afternoon
> while assisting her husband unload buffalo he had just
> purchased. The ranch foreman, Dan Silvercloud
> reported that Mrs. Smith was standing near the top
> rail of the loading shoot. She slipped and fell into
> the animal's path after releasing the pin to the discharge
> gate. Mr. Smith tried valiantly to save his wife but
> was unable to do so.

It was less than a week following the funeral that Sheriff Brinkle summoned Eddy Gavolin to his office. He had asked that Eddy bring a signature of his Grandpappy Gavolin.

The pressure of the lignite discovery, the confrontation

with Les Smith over the boundaries, and the upcoming battle with Thomas Drake, was building inside him. Not to mention the death of Sonya, the deed, and discovering the identity of his father. He was nervous, his guts felt like Jello one minute, like a rock the next. He seemed to be losing his desire for sex. He yearned to see Gloria. If he could just hold her. He was getting high on alcohol quite often now.

Checan was worried about him and was usually by his side.

The sheriff motioned for them to be seated and pitched a bill of sale toward Eddy. "Les is giving me hell about this. He says he bought the property between ya'll. He wants me to throw your ass off. Did you bring your grandaddy's signature?"

Eddy handed it to him.

He studied the two signatures. "Sure as hell don't look the same but I'm going to get a hand writing expert involved."

Eddy was hesitant but handed him the deed.

Sheriff Brinkle unfolded and studied the instrument. Then looked up to the youth, "Damn Eddy, this looks like the original deed. Where did you get it?"

"Dan Silvercloud gave it to me. Les Smith had told his mother to burn it, but she didn't."

"You think he stole the original from the county records?"

"Be my guess."

"Can you tell him you can't verify the signature on the bill of sale but don't tell the old SOB about the original deed till I tell you." He paused, and looked at the lawman. "When he finds out about that deed he will run my family off the Flying S."

"What you mean by that?"

Checan lovingly squeezed his arm.

"Dan Silvercloud is my daddy."

23

We owned it now, but Eddy remembered it had been exactly one year ago that he had driven to the Drake Hotel to meet Checan Martin. He had spent his last six dollars putting gas in a borrowed vehicle and shameful that he didn't have the money to buy her breakfast.

Now it had all seemed like a dream. He had gone to bed broke, and with Checan's help, woke up with an unbelievable pile of prosperity. Even though he didn't own cows or a ranch for them to poop on, he had formed his own company, Gavolin Land & Cattle Company. He had now sold most of his ranch with the exception being some non-lignite producing property up north on the river. He planned to develop that into a recreational area. Possibly for his own recreation. He also had signed the contract, and had received a large down payment on his half of the Flying S.

He had bought the Drake Hotel, changed the name to Sonya, and both he and Old Mose had moved in. He had sold the truck farm and the money was available with the exception of one stipulation. That being, the city of San Sonora must zone the property for commercial use.

Thomas Drake had been lividly pissed off when he returned from Las Vegas with his Arab buddy to find that Eddy had not only bought the Ripley property but his hotel as well. While he had spent the last few weeks sucking up to "Ahab" in an effort to secure drilling rights from his friggin father in Saudi Arabia. Those efforts had not yet succeeded, but in the meantime, he had let the half-breed sneak in, buy the old Drake Hotel and screw up his office and motel construction next door to the new shopping center.

Along with Todd Muhler and Jed Jutman, a good lawyer and a private detective, they would do battle with the brash young bastard. They had influenced the municipality to incorporate the property into its city limits and would now get it zoned residential instead of commercial. That would definitely chap the half-breed's butt.

The zoning commission had already done some brown-nosing and voted in favor of it, but the final outcome would be at the discretion of the city council. That would rule out a shopping center. And they had also stirred up downtown merchants to oppose it because it would be competitive to their businesses.

But actually it was Drake and Muhler that was out for his blood. They would stomp his behind publicly, and if they succeeded, he would have to eat that fancy shopping center that they themselves had envisioned.

The auditorium filled to overflowing. Seemed that half the residents had turned out to observe the encounter. They expected to see a fight and many thought the youth would be taken advantage of.

Eddy was high as usual. Without the alcohol surging through his bloodstream he would have felt uncomfortable and nervous. Instead, he felt calm and ready, and not knowing the exact reason, had donned a colorful Indian headband.

Their speeches would be almost identical, each opposing the other.

Jed Jutman, local real estate broker, and front-man for Thomas Drake and Todd Muhler, shifted his well dressed obese body behind the podium. He was the last of the three to speak. "Ladies and Gentlemen," he glanced across the audience. "These two fine business men," he paused and pointed toward them. "Thomas Drake, a very successful oil man, and Todd Muhler, a resident of San Sonora and owner of Muhler Avaition, and I might add, his aircraft manufacturing company is the biggest employer of local residents in this area. They both have advised you of their desires to see the property in question zoned residential. And we have heard from the head of the Merchants Association that this zoning would be in their best interest. And these fine gentlemen have expressed my sentiment exactly." He cleared his throat, "one short note." He retrieved a piece of paper from his coat pocket and unfolded it. "It's been rumored that Mister Gavolin has been involved in drugs. We have hired a Dallas private investigator and he reports the other person involved in this voting amendment has a suspicious background. She, at one time, worked for an escort service, which as you know is closely related to prostitution." He had not really wanted to make this accusation but Thomas had pushed him to do so.

Eddy's body became tense.

Jed Jutman did not look up. "It's rumored that this lady associated with Gavolin and Martin Investments Company has had a suspicious background involved in some of her real estate transactions." He was to get this over with. "Thank you" and he scooted his big behind from the podium and plopped down beside his obese wife.

This would be the final chapter of her book, Checan Martin thought as she arose to defend Eddy Gavolin.

Eddy jerked her back into her chair, stood up and moved his muscular body toward the podium. His long black hair flowed from beneath the beaded headband. His white t-shirt spotless, taunt over his upper torso. His jeans faded but clean. His boot heels moving close to the floor because of his slight inebriated condition. His devilish good looks and his recent introduction to a sound financial situation caused many housewives in the audience to swoon.

Eddy stepped behind the podium and looked out across the crowd. He felt good.

Surprising himself, he asked the audience to bow. He said a short prayer. He asked that his Grandpappy Gavolin would look down on him from Heaven and lead him in a direction he would have him go. He offered thanks to the Father and the Son for their compassion. He asked for guidance and leadership for the members of the council as well as all people involved. He asked that sins committed by those present, as well as his own be forgiven. "Amen."

An eerie quietness fell over the chambers as Eddy spoke. "Thank you." Now down to business. "I think most of you know me. I was born and raised out in the county on a sheep ranch and went to school here in town. If you were involved in FFA, you might remember I showed a few sheep. If you were involved in watching football, I use to kick it around a little bit."

"Go git um, Kicker," rang out from the crowd.

Eddy looked up and smiled. He knew who it was. Nobody ever called him Kicker but the assistant coach who had recruited him from the church soccer field.

The mayor chastised the intruder.

Eddy looked over at Jed Jutman. "Sir, you have made some serious accusations about my associate Miss Martin. She has been spending some of her time here in San Sonora. I'm sure you have seen her and would agree, she's a great looking woman. I know you have had some real estate dealings with her. You mentioned the word prostitute. Did you try to hire her for prostitute purposes while trying to buy property from her?"

The broker's jowls reddened as he embarrassingly shook his head.

"Do you know anybody personally who has?" He paused and pointed at the investigator. "Including your hired hand sittin there. And please answer the question, sir, so the council can hear."

He answered reluctantly, "Nope." He was sweating profusely. The kid was making an ass out of him, and Drake was sitting there like a tub of guts letting the Indian embarrass hell out of him. He should intervene on his behalf. After all he had been the one that had hired him to investigate her.

"It appears to me, Mister Jutman, if you ain't done it, and don't know anybody that's done it, in order to sway this vote, that you might be trying to blow smoke up somebody's rear end."

Some people giggled. The mayor banged his gavel.

Eddy was on a roll and realized he had help. He turned to the oilman. He noticed his wife had not joined him. "What about you, Mister Drake? You're one of the richest men around here. You could certainly afford it. Have you propositioned Miss Martin, or do you know anybody who has?"

Thomas did not move. A cold burning hatred flashed from his eyes.

"Mister Drake evidently don't like me much. When I was a kid, Mama brought me up here to his fancy new hotel. When we walked in that big ole atrium my eyes were as big as doughnuts and my heart was thumping like crazy. I thought I was going to ride that fancy elevator up to the top. But you know what, the manager wouldn't let me ride it. I reckon it was cause I looked country and dark skinned." He looked over at the wildcatter. "You remember that, Mister Drake? I think you might have been present."

His nostrils flared as Thomas Drake bolted from his chair. "What the hell's that got to do with it, Mayor?" He pointed at the mayor. "You all need to vote and get this crap over with."

The mayor was irritated and intervened. "Have a seat Thomas and let him finish his presentation. Opposition had their chance."

Eddy pointed at the investigator. "Mister Drake said something about crap. If I accused you of being full of buffalo crap, and didn't have proof to back it up, it could be a lie." He couldn't believe he said that. The alcohol must be putting words into his mouth. "Ain't that right sir?"

The audience giggled again. Even the mayor smiled.

Eddy would put his cards on the table, and gamble he was not screwing up. "If you have proof, sir, of Miss Martin ever having questionable real estate dealings or accepting money for sex, would you present it to the council."

They looked to him for an answer.

"It could be a rumor."

Eddy couldn't resist. "Then I suppose it could be a rumor that you are full of buffalo crap." He gazed across the crowd till he spotted Dave Brinkle. "And I guarantee you, it would only be a rumor if you heard that I am involved in drugs." He pointed to the ex-sheriff. "Your new county judge there is my Godfather. And I promise you, if I was, he would whup up on my brown ass."

There was a loud applause.

Thomas Drake was furious.

The Mayor had never heard this kind of talk at a city council meeting before but decided to allow it. He asked for a vote. The council voted six to two in Eddie's favor.

Eddy was elated. He could get his money now from that Dallas company for the Mose Ripley property and they could start building the River Edge Shopping Center.

24

*E*xcept for an isolated area on the river at the back side of the ranch, it was established that the richest and deepest bed of lignite lay directly beneath land which had belonged to Eddy Gavolin.

Also, the property Checan had purchased was full of the rich mineral that lay buried under the surface. It was presumed that a big portion of the Flying S would have a bountiful supply. Definitely it was deep to within two hundred yards of the ranch house. There was a fence there now, built by the mining company. Fortunately, the only thing that Les had built on Gavolin property was cowboy houses. They were vacant now. The only help he had now lived in the bunkhouse and at 72, Hooch was back at being the head honcho. Dan Silvercloud and his Uncle Dave had resigned and moved their families to town before the deed officially reappeared at the records building. Eddy had seen to it that the old rancher had not had the privilege to kick them off.

The ex-foreman, with Checan's help, was now head of security for the mining company and his uncle Dave was his assistant. In the future, they assumed they would be back on the place, but working under very different circumstances.

With the exception of half the Flying S, Checan's company had handled the sale of most all the existing lignite producing properties in the area. She had sold thousands of acre feet of the valuable black stuff. And she had made thousands and thousands of dollars without having to compromise her "ace in the hole."

That was a good thing, though, because Eddy had enticed Lambert to come to work for him, and she had developed a passionate relationship with him. And even a more weird relationship, was her older sister, Mary Bee. She seemed to be getting sweet on Les Smith. And if she was to leave the company that would create a large void. She had been spending much of her time in San Sonora, and needed her big Sis to ride herd on her Dallas office, not on Les Smith's cows. But what the hell, she could sell her Dallas firm to Jim and spend the rest of her days out here in the Southwest. And even though she didn't need the money, there was plenty of real estate activity going on in the area. And she didn't want to just sit on her butt. She also needed to keep her eye on Eddy and help him invest his money wisely. And in her opinion that helicopter he was trying to buy from Muhler Aviation was a pure waste. He had taken up skydiving and she worried he would get his brown ass killed. At first she tried to be his lover, then his mother. Now she could relish the fact that he was her best friend. And thanks to his discovery of lignite, and her speculating on the large acreage across the tracks, she was now a rich woman. And the prestigious recognitions she had yearned for among her peers in Dallas real estate seemed of little importance to her now. She seemed content just trying to make Eddy and Lambert happy.

One of the properties Checan had not handled was the land across the county road from the sheep ranch. Thomas Drake and Todd Muhler had rushed in and bought it when Eddy had turned Thomas down while the rig was still burning. They anticipated a huge profit. Actually, they should have drilled a few test holes, because when the mining company started drilling they determined that there wasn't much lignite there. It seemed abundant under the county road, but across it, it started tapering off. Now they were stuck with a lot of land and very little coal. The company was interested in buying coal producing land only, and did so. Now they had Jeb Jutman trying to sell the rest.

Eddy had a yearning for it now that he had created the Gavolin Land and Cattle Company. Unfortunately, he didn't own any land or cattle. Even though he would have an opportunity to buy the ranch back when the coal was harvested, he needed property now. And it would be years before his place became available for buy back. The property across the county road that was non-producing would suit his needs just fine. Now he had Checan trying to buy it for him. Thomas Drake hated his guts and if he found out that Eddy was a potential buyer, hell would be freezing over before he would sell it. But he had confidence in Checan and figured she could outsmart the oilman. She did.

And fortunately, the mining company had not sold his old house yet, but the house movers had it on blocks, ready to move. He would ask Checan to buy it. Then he would move it across the road. He would then buy him a few sheep, a few old longhorns, and a few donkeys. And he would need some horses. Possibly his mother's horse as well as his own pony might still be around. If he could find them, he would buy them back. He remembered his granddaddy's big horse and the old man sitting astride him. That was one fine horse. Tears formed in his eyes as he wondered if the animal was in heaven with him. He sure hoped so. He would ask Brother Rob.

Checan had obtained a contract and escrow money for Eddy's half of the Flying S, but before doing so, Eddy had met with Jake Wilson and paid him in full for the loan. He offered to sell some of his bank stock to Eddy while he was there. Eddy bought it. Jake was sure getting old. Actually they would run his old butt off if he was not the bank's biggest stockholder. He should spend more time hanging out with him. He decided to invite him to move to the Sonya. He and Mose could get together after the evening meal and spin some tall tales about the good old days. They were both moving slower and Eddy realized they would soon need medical care. When that time came, he would hire them a nurse. He was deeply indebted to both of them and would see to it they were taken care of.

The half-breed was now in position to tell Les Smith he had bought Miss Dora's half of the Flying S Ranch from the Baptist church. He could ask Mary Bee to do it but felt it was his responsibility. He dreaded it. It would surely hurt the old man deeply. But after the property line and fence building encounters, he actually should get enjoyment out of telling him. But he had forgiven the old rancher and would not enjoy it unless he remembered his responsibility for his grandpappy's arm. If that came to his mind during their conversation he might have to slap the old coot.

Uncle Dave had told him the details of that incident, showed him the gravesite. But as in his grandpappy's words, "Love thy neighbor." But that might be pushing too far. He didn't hate Les Smith but he sure didn't love him either. Next time he visited Brother Rob he would get his opinion on that also.

Eddy seldom left the area, but visiting Brothers Rob's church had become a monthly event. He had created a drug dependency fund there in Sonya's memory. That was probably his largest non-business expenditure. But he had felt gratitude to the church for the personal loan they had made to him when things were really tight. But that gratitude was only half the reason. The other half was he had acquired a case of the hots for Sister Rosilee and was trying to impress her. She was already rich so therefore his money was meaningless to her. To him, she did seem to express some interest in his visits. But Brother Rob never let her out of his sight. Eddy just couldn't comprehend that situation, but at least she was teaching him to sing. And Brother Rob was teaching him to preach. He realized he needed the preaching lesson more-so than the singing lesson, but that old Devil seemed to think otherwise. What Eddy really wanted was to...

True to his word, Eddy was helping Butch and Sundance build their energy free habitat over on the river. He had spent a small fortune helping with their semi-underground house, wind turbines, solar collectors, and methane digester. And that damn digester was a straight waste of money. By the time they hauled in enough manure from the feedlot to run it, they could buy propane cheaper. After all, gas was gas. Their methane would come from cow crap, and propane from dinosaur crap.

Eddy Gavolin had been blessed. He had been blessed financially, mentally, and physically. And since his visits with

Sister Rosilee and Brother Rob he had almost quit drinking. His life finally seemed to be coming together. He had almost finished remodeling the old Drake Hotel. He spent much of his personal time on that project. He had opened up the old lobby to the public and now people could walk through. The oil derrick replica elevator had been modernized. That had been a priority, and now any youngster walking through was welcomed to ride up to the fourth level. Often, Eddy himself would do the honor for the youngsters by riding up with them.

He had rented studio and office space to one of the local radio stations. Their location, the old check-in desk area overlooking the street as well as the walk-thru atrium. The restaurant in the hotel was holding its own but not showing a large profit. That was not a big deal for Eddy. Perhaps if he had retained the Driller, a private club created by Thomas Drake it would make money but he had rather just do without. He needed a place to eat, not drink.

Next door to the Sonya he had bought a clothing store and named it Gavolin's. He would try and compete with the big names out in the new shopping center, which was almost complete.

Unfortunately, Jimmy Muhler had not been as fortunate as Eddy. He had the opportunities available to him, but had not made the best use of them. Cocaine had been his downfall. His lack of dedication had prevented him from becoming first string quarterback his sophomore year at Texas Tech. He could not see his chances improving for the next season. A Navy Air Corps recruiter visited the campus, and after acing the test, joined the Navy. He would complete O.C.S. and become a hot shot Navy pilot. Being blasted off the deck of an aircraft carrier and doing power rolls in that big powerful fighter jet would be a lot of fun. Unfortunately, that didn't happen. Instead, his training was, lifting slowly and vertically off the deck in a Navy Helicopter. He was disappointed, but he wore the gold wings. His Dad would be proud. And Todd Muhler was proud until he received the news his son had been kicked out of the Navy. Undoubtedly drugs played a major roll.

Now Jimmy and Gloria had returned to San Sonora and both went to work for Muhler Aviation. Jimmy would sell aircraft, and Gloria took an office position.

Eddy had heard they were back.

The Sonya Hotel renovation was almost complete. He had spent a ton of money on the project and realized he could have probably built a new motel out on the highway for what it was costing. There was a new beige stucco exterior, as well as a new pool. The building still contained its original four stories, as well as the penthouse. But he had delegated the bottom floor to lease out as office space. He occupied one of the offices and lived in the penthouse. Therefore he could now live at the top and go to work at the bottom. He could eat, sleep, and work in the same building. Sounded boring as hell to him. He missed the country living he enjoyed as a kid, but the penthouse was not half bad. The carpenters, plumbers and painters were putting the final touch to it. The deck and jacuzzi were almost complete. He was standing at the door watching, waiting for it to fill with water. He remembered when he had jerked Mrs. Drake in the water tank. Things were sure different then. And then he smelled her. The aroma had won the battle over the sawdust and fresh paint. It was the same perfume he had complimented her on during the trip to her house for a fruitless meeting with Thomas Drake.

He turned and looked at her. She was immaculately dressed and looked more beautiful than ever. "I recognized the perfume."

"I hadn't forgotten how much you liked it."

He realized seeing her would once again turn his life upside down. "What in the world are you doing here?'

"Do I get a hug?"

She felt so good, so delicate. He wanted her.

She released him and took his hand. "Looks like you are doing a lot of work here, Eddy."

"I reckon this is where I'm going to live until they get the coal out from under the old ranch." He squeezed her hand. "Can I show you around?"

"I'd like that."

He led her around the interior of the sparsely furnished apartment, pointing, and explaining. He showed her the deck and the hot tub, then took her to the balcony overlooking the pool.

"That's something new, isn't it?"

"I built it for you in case you ever wanted to bring the kids over to go swimming."

She paused and then asked, "What kids?'

"You were pregnant last time I saw you."

Finally, she said, "I miscarried, Eddy."

He felt really bad. He had heard that they had moved back to San Sonora, but knew nothing about the family situation. He took both her hands. "I'm sorry, Gloria."

"It's okay, I'm not sure Jimmy was ready to be a daddy."

Eddy didn't want to pursue that subject. He might tell her just how stupid he thought Jimmy really was. "What are you over here for?"

She glanced at him, "Hoping for a favor."

"All you got to do is ask."

"Heard you had taken up skydiving."

"More fun than riding wild bulls."

She grinned, "You're probably right about that. I've tried it myself while in Corpus. It was a lot of fun."

"You and Jim come to the airport Sunday afternoon and teach me how it's done."

She squeezed his hands. "I am so proud of you, Eddy." She wondered why she had chosen Jimmy over him. But in her heart she knew. At the time, that was the way things were supposed to be. Now, things were much different. The drugs had brought Jimmy down and Eddy was on his way up.

"What kind of favor can I do for you, Gloria?"

She looked at him. His hypnotic eyes, big and bright and burning. He could talk with his eyes. He could express his thoughts, his feelings and his desires through them. He was not wearing a shirt. She looked at his chest. His light bronze skin and muscular shoulders created an eerie magnetic pull within her.

"Did you know that Jimmy is selling aircraft for his dad now?"

"Ought to be good at it."

"Did you know that I am working in the office?"

"Nope, didn't know that either."

"Did you know you were talking to me when you called the office Friday about the Sikorsky?"

He grinned, "You're kidding."

"I didn't tell you who you were talking to because I wanted to look at you while we had this talk."

Eddy figured it was favor time. He just hoped it didn't involve that sorry-assed Jimmy Muhler, but had a suspicion it would. That would be all right because he worshiped her. If it was possible for him to do it for her, he would do it.

"You didn't come over here to sell me a helicopter, did you?"

"Actually, I would like to send Jim over to talk to you about it. His dad got stuck with it when my dad suggested he rebuild it for this Arab fellow. Unfortunately, they both got screwed and got caught holding an empty bag. He headed back to Saudi, and now they can't touch him. He stuck Jim's dad for the aircraft, and my dad for a big bill in Las Vegas. Needless to say there is some friction between our families now. Unfortunately, you had something to do with that when you bought the shopping center property."

"Hope I didn't cause any problems for you."

"No problems for me. They should have stuck to the U.S.A. Dad should have stuck to the oil business here and Todd should have stuck with building and selling airplanes here also. Neither needed the money. Guess they just wanted to try something different by sucking up to a big-shot Saudi for business purposes."

She was sweating and Eddy asked if she would like to move to an air conditioned area. She preferred that no one see her with him. Jimmy would go ape if he thought she was talking to Eddy. Actually she had visited with Lambert and he had smuggled her in. "Can I tell Jimmy to talk to you about the helicopter?"

"Tell him to call me. I would like to look at it."

"You will like it. It's got a couch, a bunk, a small galley, and a polished brass water closet if you need to pee. And to

top that off, the walls are covered with thick camel hair rugs."
She touched his shoulder and grinned. "Don't worry, the interior
doesn't smell like a camel."

"How do you know what camel hair smells like?"

She laughed. "You got me there." "There's a side door
that would be great for jumping and a small door separating the
cabin from the cockpit, to give you privacy in the cabin with your
lady friends."

"You know you are the only lady friend I'll ever have. I'm
just waiting on you to dump Jimmy."

"I made my own bed, Eddy. I feel obligated to sleep in it a
while longer."

"You know I love you."

"You should hate me, but I realize now, it should have
been you."

"It's not too late."

"Jim really needs me now, Eddy."

"I'll be here for you if you ever need me," he said.

She skirted the subject. "If you buy it, will you hire Jimmy
to fly it? It wouldn't have to be full time. He could sell airplanes
the rest of the time. Flying is his life."

Eddy was curious. "Why doesn't he fly for his dad?"

"You have to be drug tested to fly for a corporation."

He was serious when he asked. "He wouldn't crash me,
would he?"

"He's a good pilot, Eddy." She hugged him. "It was good
to see you, Eddy." On the way to the doorway she turned. "He
really is a good pilot."

25

Dave Brinkle would relinquish his county judge position and was running for State Representative. His chances would be good because he had Eddy campaigning vigorously for him. And Eddy's bloodline would be beneficial because in his district there was a large Indian constituency.

Lambert Snodgrass was now Eddy's top assistant. And much to his surprise, he had married Checan Martin. On top of that she was pregnant and they were both very happy. They had gotten tired of living in the hotel and had moved into the old ranch house which had now been relocated on the property across the road. They both enjoyed country living. Checan had just about retired and had redecorated the downstairs. But at Eddy's request, she left the upstairs just as he had left it.

He often came for an overnight visit, and sleeping there definitely brought back some memories. He tried to remember only the good ones. He was very close to his mother, and a portrait of her hung prominently on the wall. But his grandpappy was his hero. He felt connected to both when he visited. It was like a ritual when he entered the room. He would first look at the picture, then the carbine which hung by the door. Then he would remove his grandaddy's Bible and the holstered forty five from the nightstand. He would gently caress the Bible before retiring. Then he would slide the pistol beneath his pillow. That Mexican sure made a big mistake when he pissed his grandpappy off.

When Eddy acquired the land across the road, he gave

the county an easement for a new road. And with their coal producing profits they had adequate profits to build a new one. Now Eddy enjoyed a new road that ran parallel to his property.

After moving the old ranch house, he had built barns, corrals and fencing, and stocked the place with a variety of animals. He had hired Dan Silvercloud's nephew to oversee the place. Actually, the whole Silvercloud family was unhappy living in the city, so he gave them land out there to build on. But instead of building, they moved in trailer houses.

And Sonya had not been forgotten. Checan had made arrangements for the rig where Sonya had died to remain in place as a memorial to her. And when the company was ready to remove the coal beneath, they would temporarily move it, and then move it back when finished. On a dark night you could see a faint glow from the flame which burned continuously at the crown of the derrick. It was fueled by propane, the same fuel that had taken her life.

The big helicopter circled the shopping center. It sure looked different now from the Mose Ripley vegetable farm. Eddy wished old Mose was airborne with them to see it from the air, but realized it would be impossible to get both his feet off the ground at the same time. When he got too old to climb the stairs to his second floor room, he assumed he would have to move his bed down to one of the offices. He had no intention of riding the elevator.

Jimmy circled steeply.

Eddy felt uncomfortable as he felt his body becoming almost parallel to the ground. He felt the turn was too steep. Then Jimmy righted the aircraft and headed southeast.

"Damn Jim, wadn't that a little steep?"

"Naw," he grinned. "I rolled one while I was in the Navy."

Eddy looked over at him. "That the reason you not in the Navy now?"

"Yep."

"Hope you won't try it in this machine."

"Want to take the controls?"

"I don't like living dangerously."

"That's B. S. Every time you strap on your chute and jump out of the belly of this thing you are taking a chance. On top of that, half the time you jump with my friends and my wife."

"Let Jordy fly and you can join us."

"That's okay, I'll fly and you all can jump. I know how much you all love it."

Eddy thought Jimmy probably was suspicious of his past feelings for Gloria. But he didn't think he realized the extent of his love. "Let's check the lake."

The company, while excavating coal, had created a large reservoir. It was customary to reclaim land after lignite had been removed. However, often excavation was less expensive than reclamation and if there was available water runoff, a lake could be created. Fortunately, run off was available from the mountain range to the west and the lake was ready for it.

The large earth moving machines were finishing the backside of the huge dam.

"Let's sit down in the bottom," Eddy said. He sure was enjoying the S1. He had nick-named it the Blue Goose just for the hell of it. Why not? Thomas had nicknamed his Lear The Silver Drake, and you sure couldn't sit the Drake down in a place like this. And it would be tough jumping from the club even at its slowest speed. Course, it would get you there faster, but Eddy seldom rushed. In his current lifestyle, he was usually in no hurry to get anywhere. And when he got there he usually was in no hurry to get back.

Jimmy circled and landed in the deepest location. "Want to get out?"

Eddy unbuckled, slid between the seats, and unlatched the small door.

When the power plant idled, he stepped through the small door and to the ground. He walked outside the prop wash and looked around. He remembered where he was standing now was some the most prime grazing space on the old sheep ranch. But all he could see now was dirt and sky. It was an unusual sight.

On the way back they buzzed Butch and Sundance. The

place was looking like a commune. They had a good field of pot growing. Eddy guessed they were using fuel for the methane digester as fertilizer for their crop. He was concerned about Butch. He just didn't look healthy.

26

Gavolin's, a newly redecorated department store, was next door to the Sonya Hotel. It had been a landmark at this location for years. Now, a different look. A western store and a stylish dress boutique had been integrated into it. Life size mannequins, male and female, adorned with the latest fashion coats, slacks, dresses, swimwear and underwear. A store where you could buy most anything from overalls to evening gowns. Their motto, "quality merchandise at discount prices." At Gavolin's the word quality and discount were bolded. Quality to compete with major brands at the shopping center, and discount to compete with the influx of discount stores being built in the Southwest.

The store was unique. A seamstress was available to alter a garment to length, over a bulging waistline or receding hips. A cobbler could conquer new soles or heels on favorite footwear. A steam machine sat ready for creasing your new cowboy hat.

On the sidewalk in front, a middle aged woman stopped to check the price of a black leather coat. A downtown secretary was admiring a bright red swimsuit as she walked by. A young Indian boy stared wishfully at a pair of western boots. Eddy spotted him on his way to the store. He stopped, smiled and asked. "What's your name?"

The youngster looked up. "Nubuck."

"You like them boots, Nubuck?"

"Sure do."

"Where is your mother?"

"In the store to buy daddy some jeans."

"Let's go in, and you can point her out to me."

After getting his mother's permission, Eddy walked with him on a shopping spree.

Nubuck really looked great in that new western shirt, boots and hat.

"Have you ridden the elevator over in the hotel, Nubuck."

 **27**

Several years had passed since Sonya had perished in the fire. In memory of her, he had integrated her name into many of his holdings. The Sonya Hotel, the Sonya Land and Cattle Company and the Sonya Ranch.

With guts, luck, sweat, heartaches and determination, this illegitimate half-breed son of a disrespected sheep woman, had carved his empire beneath the skies of Southeastern New Mexico. An empire with its buried Black Sunshine pouring into the many railcars which now dotted the horizon. And across the new county line road was the Sonya Ranch. It was now stocked with sheep, buffalo, and a hundred or so longhorns, along with a dozen wore out cow horses. He could never locate his pony but possibly he had just bought the son of his mother's horse. He was about half mean at first but when Dave's nephew had finished breaking him, he had a whole new attitude.

It was evident that prosperity existed, but there seemed to be no abundance of happiness in the youngblood's life.

Over on the backside of the ranch, the lake was now full of sparkling clear water that had cascaded down from the mountains during the spring thaw. Cold and refreshing to a bikini clad ski enthusiast as she bounced across the waves near the earthen dam. Two ardent fishermen looked at her. Then cursed as their boat rocked.

And at the site of the old Gavolin barn and corral, where many a sheep had toiled and pained with birth, another form of painless birth was being implemented. A caesarean birth from within the belly of Mother Earth. First the incision was made. Then a sound like thunder as blasters set their charges to break up the black seam of lignite. The instrument, a mammoth shovel, removed the coal and loaded the newborn product onto awaiting haulers. It was then transported to the crusher. Then to the hoppers, which sat astraddle the railroad tracks. Beneath the hoppers, a mile long train would stop and download tons of the coal before making the trip to Central Texas. There, a generating plant would consume the New Mexico coal and produce enough electricity to save millions of cubic feet of precious natural gas.

With the exception of the lake, the incision would be closed. Contoured and re-surfaced with topsoil, reseeded with grass, and would be sold. Usually to the original owner if he or she offered a competitive price. And Sonya Land and Cattle had already purchased the lake and land around it. And now that Eddy owned the lake and the non-coal bearing timberland to the river, he had planned to build a hunting and fishing lodge. That would probably piss Butch and Sundance off, because the local game warden would be hanging out in that area, and they would have to clean up their act. But Butch had not been feeling well and Eddy continued to worry about him.

Things sure had changed since Eddy was growing up out on the sheep ranch. He could remember when he was just learning to drive the old farm truck, about twelve or thirteen, and he found a nudie magazine hid under the seat. He knew it was Lester's, so he stole it, and hid it under his mattress. That was his introduction to naked women and even though he felt a little guilty, he sure enjoyed it. Unfortunately, springtime had arrived and he realized it was getting mattress turning time. And if his mom found that magazine, she would for sure whip his little butt and then burn it. What he did was tear out a page to carry to school and show his buddies, and buried the rest in the sheep barn. That one page vanished at school before a cat could lick his behind and the rest vanished that night. It didn't rain that often in that part of the state, but this was an exception. Sheep and water ran into the barn that night and the next morning his nudie magazine was disintegrated and buried beneath six inches of mud and manure. And to him that sure seemed an awful lot of punishment for such a little sin.

It seemed things were different now. Back then the models were usually porn, pros or hos. However posing nude in today's standards was not nearly as demeaning as it had been when he got his hands on that first magazine. Even some movie stars would jump naked and pose. And a new slick paper men's magazine *Pore Boy* had intentions of taking advantage of that situation. And along with a little fiction, they would feature sex, satire, sensationalism, and success. And the success section is where Eddy Gavolin had entered into the equation. Each month they would write a "Rags to Riches" tribute to the success of an American citizen. And even though Eddy had agreed to the interview, he couldn't figure out where in the hell they got his name. He suspected Checan might know something about it.

"Ahab the A.H. Arab," as he was referred to by Thomas Drake and Todd Muhler, had fled back to his own country to hide behind his daddy's coat tail. He had summoned his Saudi father to send his large private jet to pick him up in the middle of the night in Las Vegas. He had slipped off leaving both of them holding the bag before either could whip his sorry ass. He had stuck the oilman with claims of receiving a lucrative drilling contract in his country, as well as a quarter million dollar bill in Las Vegas. Todd Muhler had not been screwed so badly but he was disappointed that he would not be selling his planes in that country. The only thing he got stuck with was a camel-hair lined Sikorsky helicopter with a solid polished brass porta-potty. His company had completely refurbished the aircraft for the Arab, but fortunately Jimmy had been able to sell the sucker to Eddy Gavolin and retrieve a major part of his dad's investment. The good part of his situation was, Ahab had deserted his personal Jordanian pilot in San Sonora and he was now employed by Muhler Aviation. He could fly anything and was the best test pilot on the company payroll.

Jimmy and Gloria had been away on business when the

call came. However, prior arrangements had been that if Jim was unavailable, the Jordanian could fly in his absence. Eddy had sent the Goose to Albuquerque to pick up the person who was to interview him.

She had spent the night in the new River's Edge Inn at the shopping center. The pilot had delivered her there after the flight. He had taken a liking to her, and had offered to pick her up the next morning and escort her to the Sonya Hotel. She had been invited there by Eddy, for breakfast.

She was much prettier than expected. He had visualized an older woman wearing spectacles. After introduction formalities, he took her brief case and invited her to the patio outside the penthouse. The area was beautiful with the early morning sunrays bouncing off the adobe exterior. The red tiled roof patio glistened with droplets of dew possibly caused by a stream of vapor from the hot tub that was slowly dissipating into the cool morning air. A steaming coffee pot was plugged into an outlet in the center of the table. It was making strange gurgling noises as she removed her recorder and turned it on.

She looked at Eddy and smiled. "Sounds like the coffee pot has had some tough times."

"Been around me too long. When I moved the old ranch house, I brought it up here with me. Can't believe it still works."

She looked around. "Is this where you live?"

He nodded. "Yeah, I live at the top and work at the bottom."

"I thought you had a big ranch."

He chuckled. "It's not a big ranch. It's a toy."

"What do you mean? You've got horses and cows, haven't you?"

He was amused. "Got about a hundred old gentle longhorns, and a few old broke down cow ponies. And about thirty good show quality sheep that I raise for the Ag kids. I give them their offspring to raise and show as their F.F.A. projects. And just for the heck of it, I got a few old buffalo."

"Sure sounds big to me."

"Might be where you come from, but ranches are bigger

out here in Eastern New Mexico and West Texas. If you don't have over a thousand head out here you ain't got much of a ranch." He paused. "I can remember when my grandpappy ran over a thousand head of sheep. And Les Smith who owned the Flying S next door ran several thousand head of cattle. I think he's slowed down some since he got so old."

"I wish I could see a ranch that big."

"He don't like me so I can't take you over there, but I can show it to you from the air."

"I want to see your place too."

"From the air?"

"Actually, I would rather drive out there."

"Would you like to see it from horse back?"

"I'd love it."

At that moment a young hotel employee delivered their breakfast. Eddy had ordered bacon, eggs, sliced tomato and a Coke. She had ordered a cinnamon roll.

"Want to split the Coke?" she asked.

She removed a camera from her briefcase. "Coffee's fine."

He refilled her cup.

"Mind if I take a few pictures?"

He had in mind removing his hat but decided against it. "Reckon that's part of it."

She walked around snapping while he was eating, then returned to the table.

"Where did you get the name Venus?" Eddy asked.

She grinned. "It's actually Sally. When I posed for the magazine they called me Venus, because I'm from Virginia. Since then, I've decided to use it."

"You posed for *Pore Boy*?"

"April edition. I was the Purty Girl centerfold." She laughed. "Two full pages of co-ed beauty and in full color."

Eddy had that edition. He could even remember the picture. She had a man's tie around her neck. He guessed he had not paid much attention to her face or her name or he would have surely recognized her. "How about that?"

"Don't worry, I'm a good writer and I'll take good care of

182

you. Are you about ready for some questions?"

He poured her another cup. "Fire away."

"Why aren't you married?"

"I just can't find the right one."

Eddy thought about Gloria. He was seeing more of her now because she was flying co-pilot on many of his excursions. Eddy didn't know if that was because she was getting her private pilot's license, or to keep Jim's nose away from the cocaine. He was getting a little worried about him. His flying was okay but he seemed to be constantly bothered about something. It surely wasn't Gloria, because as far as Eddy could tell, she was truly committed. However, she did smile often now and was unusually friendly when they jumped. And if not for her, he would be more concerned about the trips to the border. They had bought a cabin down there and often borrowed the Goose for the trip. But he did trust Gloria and would do anything for her.

"Maybe someday."

"Anything you want to talk about?"

"Not really."

"Don't worry, with your good looks and money you'll find the right girl."

"Thanks for the compliment."

"And with all that money, you must be one of the happiest people around."

"Not really. Maybe you can buy contentment, but not happiness. Earlier in life I thought money could buy happiness but I have been proven wrong on a few things. That's one of them."

"Growing up on the sheep ranch, you never were that poor, were you?"

"Naw, but after I got older I got my tail in a gigantic financial crack. Couldn't even afford to buy a lady friend of mine," he pointed down at her empty plate, "a cinnamon roll for breakfast."

"Tell me about it."

"It's a strange story. I was driving a borrowed car and completely broke when my preacher loaned me twenty thousand dollars. That should have got me by for a while, but I spent it the next day on a little old piece of property. Actually it's out there where you spent the night last night."

"You mean the River's Edge Inn?"

"Yeah, that along with where the shopping center is built."

"You own that too?"

"Naw, had to sell that property because I was so broke. The lady I was coming over here to see, the one I couldn't afford to buy her breakfast, she was in the real estate business and sold it for me." He paused. "By the way, she loaned me a few thousand till things got better. Her name is Checan. You'll meet her before you leave. She's the greatest friend I ever had."

She checked the recorder. "What's your favorite hobby?"

"Use to be skiing. Tried riding a few bulls. Now it's parachuting."

"Out of airplanes?"

"Sometime we use a plane, sometime we jump from the Goose. Want to jump with us sometime?"

She grinned and motioned over her shoulder. "Only place I would be interested in jumping into is your hot-tub."

"Have at it."

"I don't have a suit."

"I could get you a tie."

"Just get me a towel."

Later in the day they drove out to the ranch. They stopped by Rayshan's to pick up the sheep dogs. Actually they were more like porch dogs. They had the proper breeding, just not the jobs. The gentle sheep Eddy owned didn't need any chasing because they never wandered far from the feed trough. When the dogs really got restless they would go out and bark at the longhorns. They didn't pay any attention to them, until they got tired of all that noise. Then they would lower those long pointed horns down to the ground and chase them off. The dogs recognized Eddy and were in the back of the truck before he could completely stop. Venus realized now why Eddy drove a pickup instead of a sports car. It probably would have never made it over the cattle guard, and if it had, there wouldn't have been room for the dogs.

Suddenly Eddy heard a loud noise from inside. He stepped out and went up to the front door, opened it and peeped in. His great Grandmammy Silvercloud was kicking hell out of the clothes washer. She was getting old and had mistakenly loaded Rayshan's dirty dishes in his clothes washer. And before she could stop it, most of them were broken. Eddy put his arm around her and led her to the couch and turned on the TV. She was mumbling something about Rayshan should get him a woman to do his damn cleaning. Eddy told her to leave everything alone and he would get it taken care of.

When they got to the barn there were two horses saddled and ready. Eddy pointed to the older horse. Venus hung the camera around the horn and hopped on.

Eddy walked his horse over to where Rayshan was working. "Better knock off what you are doing out here and go to the house. Mammy's plenty pissed off cause she done broke the biggest part of your dishes in the clothes washer."

He smiled and shook his head.

She sure enjoyed the ride as well as getting some great pictures of the ranch. Eddy had warned her. Now she was already getting sore. By morning she would be walking bow-legged. She was happy her editor would not see her walk. He would surely accuse her of too much hanky panky with the Rich Dude. And she sure had enjoyed visiting with Checan and Lambert. Checan had bragged that Eddy was the greatest person in the world. Lambert didn't go that far, but said he was the best and fastest damn derrick man who ever rode an elevator to the top of a drilling rig. Then he bragged that he had a hell of a teacher.

Eddy had called, and now the Goose was landing outside. All the animals, with the exception of the sheepdogs, were heading for the north forty. The dogs were ready to fly.

Jordy had come to pick them up and Venus was happy about that. She just hoped she could walk straight legged to the aircraft.

Eddy opened the small entry door and the dogs jumped in.

Venus had wanted to photograph Eddy jumping, so after boarding, he slipped his jeans and shirt off and got into his jump suit. He then strapped Venus into a safety harness. He slid the communication mike and phones onto her head and hit the switch. "Don't say anything you don't want Jordy to hear."

She smiled. "Are you there Jordy?"

"Roger."

Eddy strapped on his chute, and then the other head-set. "Okay Jordy, we are ready to roll back here. She wants some pictures of the Flying S from the air. Take it slow and easy over the house and barn and then show her a bunch of his old cows. Then a few deer. She will like that."

"Roger that. I'm moving up."

The twelve hundred fifty horsepower turbine engine roared to life and the helicopter soared into the air. Eddy handed her the camera and slid the belly door open.

She was worried about the dogs and pointed toward them.

"You couldn't throw them out." Eddy said.

She could already see the Flying S. It was a gorgeous panoramic view of breathtaking beauty. She recognized the large ranch house, the windmill, the corals, and the barns. She was snapping pictures when she asked, "What's that little house sitting out behind the house with the smoke coming from the side of it?"

Eddy laughed. "The big house is the bunkhouse. The smoke is coming from the outdoor kitchen, and the two little houses out back are outhouses. One for Hooch and Pooch and the other for the ranch hands. Bet you never peed in one of them before."

"Have you?"

"Actually, we had indoor plumbing on the ranch. On the rig we had one of them metal ones, but it didn't get much use if there was a mesquite bush around."

She laughed as Jordy circled in front of the large old battered ranch house. Eddy was peeping over her shoulders and realized if Missus Smith was still alive the house would have a fresh coat of paint.

"Great, great pictures," she muttered.

He then headed across the Flying S range land. She had never seen so many cattle.

"Where to next, Boss?"

"Let's check the lake, the mining operation, and then the derrick. I don't have an aerial picture of it. Take it in close and let Venus get a couple pictures there. Then back to the ranch, I guess." He paused and thumbed his straps, "She wants to see me jump. Take me over the house at about fifteen hundred. I'll jump, open and you can circle and she can get my picture."

"Roger that. Good luck."

28

There were two categories. Junior Miss, thirteen through sixteen, and Senior Miss, seventeen through nineteen. It was a beauty and talent contest and you must be attending, or had graduated from San Sonora High. It had been sponsored by the Downtown Merchants Association. It would be an all day affair in an effort to steal customers from the new shopping center out on the river. The talent competition had been held in the school auditorium. Apparel modeling competition was in the school cafeteria where a catered meal was served. That had cost the local merchants a bundle since the contestants got to keep the clothing they modeled. Later in the afternoon the Junior Teen evening gown and swim suit competition was held at the city pool. Because of Eddy Gavolin's generosity, and the fact that some members were curious to see the new remodeled Sonya Hotel, association members suggested the hotel pool for the final competition. And unfortunately for him, that got him as well as Checan a judge's spot. Other judges were Damond Silvercloud and the local home-making teacher. Damond was quite a celebrity now. He had been drafted by a professional football team and hoped to be traded to Dallas.

Earlier that day, several members of the club jumped from the Goose near the school. Jimmy Muhler had used that opportunity to tell Eddy that Gloria's sister Ronda would be competing that evening at the pool. "Do you know her?"

"Met her once." Eddy remembered the Jeep ride. "When

she was a kid, but I probably wouldn't know her now."

Because of Eddy's success, Jimmy really disliked Eddy now, but he had a need for him. He needed to fly, and he needed drugs. Eddy helped provide both, because of the Goose.

"She's all grown up now, and beautiful." He had wished Eddy could meet her, and develop a relationship with her. If that happened maybe he could keep those lustful Indian eyes off his wife. "I would like to introduce you to her tonight."

"I'll reserve you a table." Eddy realized Thomas Drake hated his guts and figured it would be futile for him to ask. He asked anyway. "Invite your in-laws."

Eddy Gavolin no longer looked like a boy. Even though he was still a young man, his face was now lined with maturity, generated not only by the circumstances of his birth, but also by his recent business dealings. Those business successes made him one of the more recognizable young men in the state of New Mexico. The fact that he had been born into the world a half-breed, a bastard, and a nobody, had been negated by his good looks, success and wealth. Now wherever he went he was pursued by daughters of the rich, and smothered with the attentions forced upon him by their scheming mercenary mamas. To them, he would be a prize catch for their precious daughters. Mrs. Thomas Drake was not an exception. She realized that something rather unusual had happened between them. It had taken that for her to realize that Eddy had really loved Gloria. But Gloria had gone with the star quarterback, shotgun wedding and all. Then lost the baby. Now, the shining star on his brow had dissipated to make more room for drug ecstasy on his brain. Perhaps it was meant to be that she lost the baby because she couldn't visualize Jimmy possibly being a great parent. Now she realized that Eddy would be a fine prospect for her younger daughter, Ronda, even though Thomas didn't like him. Possibly they could reconcile if he became a family member, and he would certainly be a prize catch for her. And certainly Eddy would be an improvement over the fast crowd at the country club.

The area was filled to capacity, and the high school jazz

band was entertaining. They were sporting their new black tie uniforms purchased by one of Checan's companies. She had also furnished a five thousand dollar scholarship for tonight's winner. An unnamed donor had matched that number. Everybody suspected that it could be Eddy Gavolin. And when he appeared, a young and beautiful girl tapped him on the shoulder. "I want to win tonight," she said. Then she disappeared quickly into the crowd. He didn't know for sure, but thought she was Gloria's little sister.

And Ronda Drake did win the competition. Not because of what she had said to Eddy, but because of her talent, personality and beauty.

Thomas Drake had agreed to let his wife sit at the table with Gloria and Jimmy. However, he would stand at the back avoiding any front row attention. He could never forget the embarrassment Eddy had exposed him to at the city council meeting. She would join him and they would leave immediately after the winner was announced. Gloria could chaperone Ronda.

The spotlights were out now and the crowd had dwindled. Only a few stragglers remained at their tables. The table that Eddy had reserved for Jimmy was getting a little rowdy. Eddy had invited Checan, Lambert, and Jake Wilson to join them. Checan had brought champagne. Jimmy had brought a bottle of booze and he and Eddy were partaking.

Eddy was in a turmoil. His desires were divided between the two sisters. One he loved, one he wanted. He needed to jump to relieve his tensions. When he was alone in the sky, floating downward to the earth. he felt contentment. He felt an unreal closeness to his maker.

"Are you sober enough to fly, Jim? I need to jump. This has been a hectic day."

Gloria took Jimmy's arm. "You are not sober enough for a night flight and he is not sober enough for a night jump. We can't afford to lose you two." She looked over at Eddy. "Go jump in the Jacuzzi, that will fix you up."

"I've got my suit in the dressing room. I'll join you," Ronda said.

"Your dad would have my scalp," Eddy replied.

"He won't know."

"Gloria would tell him."

"You won't tell him, will you, Sis?"

Gloria looked over at her little sister. "I won't tell." Now she was jealous. "Have fun."

"We'll wait on you," Jimmy said. His plan was coming together.

Ronda grabbed Eddy's hand and they took off.

In the hot tub Eddy refused Ronda's offer of her virginity. He lectured her on her good fortune and advised her of the importance of keeping her body pure until marriage. And when they returned to the table she whispered in Gloria's ear, "The butthead wouldn't do me. Then he gave me a sermon."

She smiled and whispered back, "Hope you listened to him."

Not hearing what the sisters were saying, Eddy congratulated Ronda again for winning, thanked her for participating, and kissed her goodnight.

It was nearly midnight now, and with the exception of Lambert, Checan, and Old Jake, the pool area was nearly deserted. The place was a mess.

29

Several months later the article on Eddy appeared squeezed in between pages of advertisements, short stories, satire, and photographs of a bevy of brazen beauties baring bosoms, backs, bellies, buttocks, and birthmarks. Lester Snodgrass had studied this array at every opportunity in the prison library, but it was not until the fifth day that he noticed the interview with Gavolin. In fact, he had to read the article numerous times to be completely convinced that this was actually the son of his once common-law wife and what he had a suspicion to be, that big Flying S Buck.

At first, he was angry at himself. Angry at the fact he had stabbed the sheep woman, received life imprisonment, and could not take advantage of that enormous amount of wealth the half-breed had come into. If not for that early morning drunken altercation it would be their money instead of his. But now, now that he had confided with his cellmate Legs Radike, he felt comfortable about the situation. They would formulate a plan and break out. Then grab the kid, collect a big ransom and head for Mexico. Lester reasoned that his part would be enough to get him a woman down there and live happily ever after. That's not exactly what Legs anticipated for him.

Lester figured on about five million, but Legs figured about half of that would be all they could possibly get together on such a short notice. And the sooner he could get across the border the happier he would be.

Legs had good contacts on the outside. He had been sent up for transporting a large quantity of cocaine. But because he divulged no names at his trial, that made him a well respected member of the organization. And the organization was tight with a Mexican drug cartel that would be helpful across the border. He was smart and would make all the necessary arrangements for the escape.

The escape plan was a bit complicated and took a few months to conceive, but if everything went to perfection it would be a breeze. His friend Rags would commandeer that big helicopter, take Eddy Gavolin and Jimmy Muhler hostage and then fly to the prison to pick them up. Most of the engineering ingenuity would be handled by him. Rags was only a nickname he had been tagged with soon after their arrival from Detroit. Rags got a job at the San Sonora airport as an aircraft cleanup contractor, and to look the part he carried a long rag hanging out his back pocket. He hated the job, not because it involved off-loading the incoming drugs, but because he had to suck up to the rich asses who owned those fancy aircraft. Part of his job was to rake out the beer cans, dust and vacuum the cigarette ashes, and discharge the contents of the pee potty. And what really ticked him off was when he had to clean up one of them damn stinky semen splotches off the lush seats. He sure as hell would like to quit, but he was being paid big money and he just couldn't afford to quit at the present time.

With an offer of enough money to retire on, Rags had reluctantly agreed to assist Legs in his escape. He would scout out the area around the prison, find a suitable landing site near the fields, and acquire suitable weapons. He would make the arrangement to commandeer the aircraft when the time came. He would be assisted in the breakout by Legs' brother and girlfriend. She was mean as hell and could hold up her end. At the present time she was his contact with Legs.

After their escape, they would swing by San Sonora to pick up their ransom and then head across the desert to Mexico. With the helicopter they could skip through the mountain passes and skim across the desert, avoiding radar detection. But Legs knew the possibility of the Feds being on their tails, but they would not shoot them down because of the hostages.

Legs had worked out the plan to perfection. And it sure would be enjoyable to see his girlfriend, brother, and Rags. And if it worked out, his friend could retire and throw that damn dirty rag he carried in his back pocket away. But if he did that he would probably need another nickname.

The plan seemed perfect.

Rags had been Jimmy's contact as well as other pilots when they brought drugs in from the border. Therefore, he didn't suspect anything when he was summoned to meet with him at the hangar. It had been quite a surprise when he arrived. Looking down a gun barrel, he was directed to summon Eddy. And the tone in Jimmy's voice convinced him to get out to the hangar immediately.

Now they were hostages, and the aircraft commandeered. A two and half million dollar ransom had been ordered. Eddy had one leg chained to the sofa, and was handcuffed to the overhead bunk. Jimmy was chained on to the pilot's seat. Eddy conceded that they were in a hellofa mess.

Before arriving at the prison, Rags had told Jimmy to call his wife and make her aware of the circumstances. Because of his dad's money and her dad's money, he took it upon himself to up the ante on the ransom an extra half million dollars. That would surely make Legs proud of him.

Gloria was hysterical when she received the call but told Jimmy she would make the arrangements.

Without lights, they landed shortly after four in the morning in a deep ravine near the prison. The girlfriend was to guard the hostages and shoot Eddy if Jimmy tried to start the aircraft.

Loaded with an assortment of weapons, a two-way radio, and wire cutters, they took off.

The prison bean field was fenced in and located several hundred yards from the prison walls. They cut a hole in the back fence and made their way to the front gate. It was getting daylight. Legs' brother camouflaged himself under the cover of the lush green bean crop. Rags, was waiting in the porta-can. It would be a long wait and it sure did stink in there.

After a couple of hours the work crew entered and the guards locked the gate behind them. The prisoners slowly off-loaded and grabbed their fiberglass bags. They would stuff them with fresh green beans, empty their harvest in the back of the truck, and go back for more.

One of the prisoners headed for the porta-can and was pretty surprised when he jerked the door open and came face-to-face with a man holding an automatic weapon. Legs pulled the man in front of him and demanded that the guards drop their rifles. Three of the guards carried rifles, the rest carried hand guns. Two of them obeyed immediately. The other swung his rifle around and stared at Rags.

Legs' brother eased out from under the cover of beans, his weapon strapped over his shoulder and a live grenade in his hand. With everyone's attention on the porta-can, he managed to move within a few feet of two of the guards before they spotted him. When the guard with the rifle saw the grenade he immediately tossed his weapon to the ground.

Rags ordered the prisoner who had discovered them to pick up the rifles and put them in his bean bag. Legs then grabbed the bag and rushed over to greet Rags. Rags handed him a loaded, light weight automatic weapon.

"You gonna be rich and retired before this day is over." Rags said to his buddy as he ordered the prisoners to start picking beans.

They had returned with two hostages, one being the guard who had been hesitant to drop his weapon. Rags had a burning desire to kick his rear end and he might just do that before he got aboard.

The only thing Lester had ever done for Legs was to show him that article in the magazine. That had given him some good ideas on the breakout, but Rags had done all the work, so he decided to leave Lester behind and give Rags his cut. He didn't think much of any man that would kill his wife anyway. Why didn't he just give her a good ass whupping?

The Blue Goose proved to be the perfect vehicle for their escape. It was roomy, and with a payload capacity of three thousand pounds, would more than accommodate the hostages, the accomplices, and the convicts. It had a good communications system and they could stay in contact with Eddy's bank as well as pursuing law enforcement. It could, with its turbo powered twelve hundred fifty horse power engine, cruise close to one hundred and fifty miles an hour. It had a flight range that could easily carry the group into Old Mexico. Its ability to land and take off vertically, and hover at a standstill would prove to be a big asset for the ransom pickup.

It had been several hours since Jimmy had done drugs, and when the phone rang that morning he had been caught cold. Now his body was beginning to ache. He desperately needed a snort, or smoke, or pills or something to relieve his tensions. Eddy noticed his nervousness. And the girlfriend suspected that Jimmy was a user and could see it in his eyes when she waved her drug paraphernalia bag in front of him. It might be a long wait before they returned with Legs, and to relieve the monotony she might have some fun with him.

His hands had not been cuffed, and Eddy could see she was going to make a fool out of him. "Knock her on her butt, Jimmy, and let's get the hell out of here."

Jimmy didn't absorb what Eddy said, but she had. Flying from the cockpit, she pushed him down on the couch. He kicked at her but she jumped on top of him.

"Go to hell, bitch."

"Kiss my ass, rich boy."

He managed to take a good bite on one of her legs but screaming, she slammed him across the head with her gun. It only stunned him but he pretended to be unconscious.

She got off him, cursing loudly, and returned to the cockpit. She needed a hit. She picked up her bag and plopped down, the gun in one hand and a syringe in the other.

She was calm now as she looked over at Jimmy. "Would you like to do a little something for me," she said with a sly smile on her face.

"You do a little something for me and I'll do a little something for you," he replied. She checked his arms. No needle marks. "Here's what you do," she said, showing Jimmy the routine.

Eddy slowly opened his eyes and watched as she inserted the same needle she had used into Jimmy's left arm. He despised Jimmy more than ever now. His weakness, his habit, and his cowardice.

Shortly after midnight Rags had called Jimmy and told him that Eddy wanted to meet him at the hangar. Gloria had not been concerned because that was part of his job as Eddy's pilot. On at least two occasions Eddy had agreed to transport critically ill or injured patients from out in the desert to the Albuquerque hospital. She glanced out the window and saw that it was a clear night. Before slamming the front door, he told her he would call later.

She went back to sleep, but at five o'clock she got the call from the helicopter. Jimmy and Eddy were being held for a three million dollar cash ransom. Fifty dollar bills or larger. They would pick the money up around nine, and if it was not ready they would kill the two.

She immediately called Checan and Lambert, then Todd Muhler.

Checan jumped into action and called Jake Wilson, then Dan Silvercloud.

Old Jake, Checan, Lambert, Gloria and Dan Silvercloud all met at the bank, along with several law enforcement officers, disbelief on all their faces.

Dave Brinkle as well as the F.B.I. had also been contacted.

Old Jake had racked his brain fruitlessly trying to come up with a way to raise the three million cash. There was another bank in town, but between the two there would be no way to come up with that kind of money.

Dan Silvercloud came up with an idea but decided to keep it to himself for the time being. But he called his brother Dave, and told him about his plan. It would be a last resort.

Rags had come up with a dramatic way to pick up the ransom. He showed Jimmy a picture of the memorial derrick that Legs had torn from the magazine. "Can you get in close enough to it for a man to toss a suitcase full of money aboard?" he asked.

Jimmy was surprised at how strong and fast the injection had worked. Soon after hitting his bloodstream, he was feeling like superman.

"No problem but I'll have to move to the other seat where I can see better."

Rags unlocked the leg chain while he switched seats.

"It would be easier without the chain."

"Don't try nothing stupid."

The bank was notified. They would want to see one man, one suitcase full of money on top of the derrick, and absolutely no vehicles in the area.

Legs Radike really felt great. This was his first hour of freedom in more than three years. He joked, laughed, and kidded as to what they would do with all that money after reaching Mexico safely. "How much longer to San Sonora?"

Jimmy turned to him. "E.T.A. twenty five minutes."

30

*J*immy slowly circled the derrick, having spotted the lone tall figure standing on the work board atop the tall metal structure. A large suitcase was at his side.

Rags quickly released the jump-seats and slid them away from the door area. He then slid the door wide open. Legs took a position near the bunk, holding a gun. His palms sweaty, his knees trembling with excitement when he saw that big suitcase.

They were all unbuckled now, excited and greedily awaiting the transfer.

Dan Silvercloud had taken control of the operation. At home, he removed his boots and jeans, and got into his fatigues. He then pulled his combat boots on and quickly laced them. He had not worn them since his discharge. They felt good. He grabbed his loaded handgun, kissed his wife and rushed out the door. His security people were waiting outside. They would be camouflaged and dug into the desert around the rig. County and state law enforcement would secure the perimeter outside the coal company's property. The large suitcase was ready, sitting in the shade near the front steps. Dave Silvercloud picked it up and gently loaded it into his company pickup. His nephew, Rayshan, would take them to the rig and then return to the office to await further instructions.

With a full tank of gas and powerful binoculars, Jordy had

reached an altitude in his fixed wing aircraft to where he would not be conspicuous to the incoming helicopter. When he spotted it, he would stay in constant radio contact with the tower.

When Dan reached the rig, he turned the gas off to the flame atop the structure. Then with Dave's help, he attached the suitcase to his shoulder harness, tied a rope around his waist, and headed to the top. Dave headed out into the desert where he would be buried in the sand with an unobstructed view.

They didn't have to wait long.

Dan's hat blew off as the helicopter circled but his eyes never lost contact with the door. His hand tightened on the handle and his thumb against the latch. He spotted Eddy on the bunk and a man pointing a gun out the door toward him. He remembered his own gun on his back. Guns seemed so useless now, failure or success rested in his hands and the pilot's ability. Damn, he was good. The big door was within two feet of him, practically no backwash at this distance. He unsnapped the latch and with all his strength hurled the heavy suitcase into the aircraft's belly.

All hell broke loose as rattlesnakes spilled out onto the floor of the helicopter. They slithered with lightning speed, striking and releasing venom into anything moving.

Jimmy was startled at the screams and jerked the helicopter away from the rig. Rags was knocked out the door and plummeted to the ground. Legs was fighting to keep his balance as the helicopter headed down. It was a hard landing. And Legs was the only one who escaped the snakes. The rest were pretty much done for with the exception of Eddy.

Legs jumped out of the cabin and started for the rig. He would kill the bastard who threw those snakes. But Dan saw him coming, his short stubby legs churning. He pulled out his gun and took a bead. "You need to drop that gun," he hollered.

"I'm going kill your ass," was the reply as he took a shot at the Indian.

Dan took careful aim and pulled the trigger.

Dave was the first of the security team to reach the aircraft.

He kicked several snakes out the door but one lay across Eddy's leg, beady eyes staring at him. He would have to be careful with that one. There was a slight grin on Eddy's face. The kid was brave. Must be that Indian blood, Dave thought. With one hand Dave grabbed the snake and swung him through the door.

"You okay, Eddy?"

"Been my lucky day near as I can tell," he replied.

37

Since the prison breakout and ransom experience, Eddy had changed. He wanted to get more enjoyment out of life. Business and success seemed less important now. He enjoyed traveling now and even though the Goose was ready, he often went by car. It all started when he had driven old Mose to visit his daughter in San Diego. He had never, until now, realized the beauty that Mother Nature had bestowed upon this earth. It had always been there but it was at this point in his life that he was beginning to notice. And one of the wonders was the Pacific. He had not seen the ocean before.

After that he felt obligated to take a trip with Uncle Jake, and the old rascal insisted they go in his Chrysler. Eddy agreed even though it was eleven years old. If they had a problem they would just buy a new one, he figured. They headed for the Ozarks and then to Hot Springs. Even the Grand Old Opry merited a visit.

Back home, he managed to take in the wonder and beauty of Carlsbad Caverns. And he even played barefoot in the great White Sands with Checan's daughter Marie.

Meanwhile, Jimmy was still pilot of the Goose. Eddy hadn't used it much lately but each time, Gloria was in the co-pilot seat. Something to do with the ransom incident, Eddy assumed. That was not a problem for him because he always enjoyed seeing her.

On one occasion Eddy called Jimmy and set up a flight to Dallas on a Sunday. The pilot's old football buddy from high school, as well as Eddy's step-brother, Damond Silvercloud, would be playing. It seemed strange to Eddy that back in the early days, Jimmy was the big star. But it had turned out much differently. That gentle giant of an Indian who had gotten a grant and scholarship to a small college was now playing football at a professional level. And the "Big Star" was now working part time for the lackluster kicker. Weird.

Damond had not started, but was playing before half time. Eddy wished he knew they were there, but seeing Gloria so happy made him feel good.

Minutes before half time Jimmy excused himself and Gloria warned him not to do anything stupid. "Just going to the can," he replied. Gloria thought otherwise.

"How are things going for you?" Eddy asked after Jimmy left.

"Seems things haven't gone well lately." She squeezed his arm. "I married him for better or for worse, but I can safely say it's getting worse instead of better."

"He hasn't tried to hurt you, has he?"

"Himself maybe, but not me. I wouldn't put up with anything like that." She looked around. "He's depressed but I think the prison incident somehow gave him a new meaning in life."

"I can understand that, and it sure got me to thinking. Man upstairs was looking out for us both that day. Hope he is smart enough to see that."

"His main problem is drugs, Eddy. I feel pity for him, and have truly tried to help him." She shrugged. "I'm about ready to give up."

Eddy wanted to tell her that he still loved her, but at that moment Jimmy came back with a Coke in each hand and was smiling.

It had been an early game and the limo Checan had arranged for them was waiting near the gate. They arrived at the airport by five and were airborne by five thirty. They circled around Fort Worth and headed west. Eddy was bored and spent much of the return trip thinking about Gloria. If he could, he should just forget her and go after her little sister.

The rays of the late afternoon sun were still spilling into the cabin as they soared above the rich irrigated West Texas farmland. Just then the buzzer sounded and Eddy picked up the mike and head set. Jimmy said Gloria had a bad migraine, and asked if she could come back and lie down on the couch. Eddy opened the door, and she eased through. He closed the door and took her arm. "Sorry you have a headache."

"Don't worry. It's just a horny headache."

Then she grabbed him, pulling him closer. Their lips met as he smelled his favorite perfume.

"I love you, Eddy, I love you," she whispered into his ear.

At that moment the cockpit door burst open and Jimmy was staring back at what he had long suspected. They had been caught with their pants down.

Eddy lunged at the door but Jimmy pulled it shut and slammed the lock down.

Eddy grabbed a headset. "What the hell do you think you are doing Jimmy?"

"That would be a question for you, Eddy," he shouted back. "After all, she's my wife."

"Why the hell don't you treat her like one?"

"Put her on the other headset." His voice trailed off. "I want to tell you both goodbye before I take us into the ground."

"What the hell do you mean, Jimmy?" Eddy shouted, jerking out two chutes.

"She knows what I mean. I told her I would kill myself if she ever looked at another man." He paused. "It's all your fault."

"Not my fault. You should have treated her right."

"I ain't never looked at another woman."

"It's not women I'm talking about. You love that coke more than her."

The aircraft jerked slightly as Eddy eased Gloria toward the door.

"Way you talking you might be going to do something stupid to her." He paused, grasping the door handle firmly in his hand. "If you do, you will for sure go to hell."

"I'll be taking both of you with me," were the last words they heard.

That was it. Eddy jerked the door open and pushed Gloria out.

Eddy felt the nose lurch downward just as he jumped. He looked around to see Gloria floating within a couple hundred yards.

The sun had disappeared beneath the horizon just as a red ball of flame erupted and leaped into the air as the helicopter crashed into the ground. Then they heard the sickening sound of the earth-jarring explosion.

Safely on the ground, they made a pact. They would tell everyone that Jimmy had advised them to put on their chutes. The aircraft had acted up and they jumped. At least half the statement was true and Jimmy would be a hero for saving the life of his wife and his friend.

32

The letter read:

Eddy,

If I stay in San Sonora, I know I could not stay away from you. And even though my heart aches to be near you, my conscience demands the opposite at this time.

I will be in Europe visiting with my mother's sister the next several months. Please do not try to contact me.

With all my love forever and forever, Gloria

P.S. I hope you will not feel responsible for Jimmy's death. It was only a matter of time.

33

The dust storm that had blown into New Mexico from the west arrived swiftly, unexpectedly, and without previous warning. And with it came darkened skies, low visibility, and hazardous driving conditions, even for the sober. But in the months since Gloria had left for Europe, Eddy's life had been an expansive void. To compensate, he drank heavily. This night was no different.

He was in his usual drunken stupor as he was driving in from Ciudad Juarez where he had entertained a group of backers engaged in Dave Brinkle's political campaign. The others had flown back aboard the charter, but since the crash of the Blue Goose he had refused to fly.

It was a dark desolate stretch of road, and Eddy had been aware of the headlamps following him. He mumbled drunkenly to himself. "That SOB has been on my butt ever since I left El Paso."

Fantasies of another extortion attempt flitted through his foggy mind. He speeded up. The car behind him did likewise. He was almost to the turnoff to Brother Rob's Half-Way House. He would take it if he couldn't shake the car behind him. He watched the speedometer needle hit 100. The car behind him drifted back. He felt more comfortable now.

Alcohol pulsated through his bloodstream.

His head pounded.

He shouted.

He sang.

He spat at the closed window and watched the mucas run slowly down the glass.

He remembered his last visit to Brother Rob's. On that occasion, he finally succeeded in getting to Sister Rosilee. He remember the brief and sensuous affair, as well as the aftermath. The aftermath had been hell. Certainly no problem from Sister Rosilee. Actually, the only time he had heard from her since was a short thank you note acknowledging the large donations he still made to the church. After he had seduced her, he could feel the presence of the devil in himself. So strong was this presence that he even made a healthy contribution to all the churches in San Sonora, and had promised to be a better person. This had seemed to quell the situation somewhat.

A drizzle began to fall and a combination of moisture and sand clung to the windshield. Eddy switched on the wipers, making things worse. He squinted through a small opening and slowed to 60. His head nodded, but he jerked it up. He forced his eyes open, but he could not long see the ribbon of pavement ahead. He responded as quickly as his drunken reflexes would react.

It was a sickening crash.

Eddy Gavolin's body was limp, and lifeless but his mind still functioned. Abnormally perhaps, because believable but unreal memories flashed before him. He saw himself as a young boy back on the sheep ranch. He was busy castrating a herd of young male sheep. Just as he positioned his razor sharp knife onto one of the sheep's testicles, it thundered and began raining blood, and hailing sheep-balls. The next day, or perhaps a month or a year, he was walking to the school bus stop when he heard the noise behind him. He turned only to see the earth open and swallow the old ranch house. It closed as abruptly as it had parted, and where the house once stood, the magnificent Evangeline Oak was now standing. Then a flaming rig appeared in his mind. It was his, and he was running desperately toward it. When he neared, there was an explosion and he watched with horror as Sonya and her kitten floated gently beneath an open parachute up into the heavens.

Time flew by. He was in town now, standing outside the bank in San Sonora. He heard the screams, turned to see the beautiful Mrs. Drake driving an old Cadillac convertible toward him. A set of long bull horns mounted onto its grill. She was smiling and waving, and Thomas was screaming and cursing. He was hanging in midair, his cowboy boots kicking for, but not reaching the ground. One of the horns was in his backside. The scene was so real Eddy's body rocked to life as he shook with laughter.

Still laughing, he opened his eyes, suddenly aware of the blinding lights on him.

Brother Rob was the first to arrive following the crash. Unknown to Eddy, he had been the tail-gater. He had stopped and to his surprise saw a lone dark figure emerging from the crumpled vehicle and walking toward him smiling. He must be drunk. No sober person could have survived unscathed.

"Howdy." Eddy's grin disappeared, replaced by surprise. "Is that you, Preacher?"

Brother Rob was surprised as well and could only ask, "Anybody else in that car with you, Eddy?"

"Nope." Eddy swung in, and dropped onto the plush seat.

"Are you all right?"

"Yup," Eddy laughed. "Less I got a dose of V D down across the border tonight."

"I'd better get you to a hospital."

"No need. I'm okay. They would just get me for a D.W.I. if you did. Just dump me at the next service station. I'll call Bert to come pick me up."

Brother Rob pulled his car back onto the highway. He could smell the whisky on Eddy's breath.

"I'm a no good bastard, Preacher."

34

When Eddy Gavolin awoke the following morning, his head was pounding. He slowly opened his eyes, sat up in bed, and threw the sheet off. Both the bed and the walls were slowly revolving. He was not alone.

"What in the world are you doing in my bed?"

"I'm trying to get your attention."

"You sure have done that." He could smell her fragrance.

She moved up beside him. "I need somebody to take care of me, Eddy."

Her face was as beautiful as ever.

"You got Brother Rob to take care of you."

"Have you thought about the possibility of it being the other way around?"

"Actually, I have," he replied.

"I do give him credit for being a gifted preacher. He has worked hard, and he's obsessed with the eradication of drug abuse. His problem, there's just too much of it for him to handle. Perhaps that's the reason he's such a blatant sinner."

Eddy thought of his Grandpappy, but he sure couldn't remember him ever doing any sinning. In his young eyes sinning was for people, not preachers.

"Is he spending too much time with some of the girls in rehab," Eddy asked softly.

"That, along with the trips across the border." She hugged him tighter. "When he takes the tapes down to the radio station, he's spending a lot more time down there than necessary."

"Why don't you sue him for half the money he's raking in out behind the church here. That would put him to thinking."

It had been over two weeks since Butch had died. He had been sickly for quite some time and AIDS had finally claimed him. His promiscuous lifestyle had brought it on. If Brother Rob could have seen his frail and bony body lying there in the casket, he might turn over a new leaf. Seeing what a few moments of satisfaction might lead to could scare the crap outta him. He might decide to quit fooling around with those young girls and ask Sister Rosilee to marry him. But that was water under the bridge. Now, they were on their way to San Sonora in Sister Rosilee's luxury car.

Before they left they had been cursed, preached to, and prayed for, to the extent that Eddy had made a promise to join a church. Brother Rob had wanted to do those honors, but Eddy balked in favor of The First Baptist Church in San Sonora. Fortunately, he had become friends with the new Baptist minister in San Sonora. That friendship had developed after he had visited several times with Butch before his death. And Sundance had promised him he would attend someday, but so far that had not materialized.

They slowed as they passed his wrecked car. When he got home he would send a wrecker to pick it up.

Eddy felt good about convincing Rosilee to leave Brother Rob. She needed more than that. Maybe her brother Sundance fit that category. And now that Butch had died, he needed someone as well.

Their first stop was the ranch where Eddy called the dealership and asked that they retrieve his wrecked automobile on Monday. Also get another one similar to it ready. He would pick it up the next day.

Later that afternoon they arrived at the house Butch and Sundance had built into the ground. She recognized that all those years of drug use had created an affliction in Sundance that needed immediate attention. And now that he had lost his best friend, she just hoped she might be instrumental in his rehabilitation. She wanted him to return to California with her where excellent doctors would be available. Sundance wouldn't agree, but didn't disagree either. They asked him to attend church the following Sunday. He didn't agree to that either.

The next morning a good crowd was in attendance at the First Baptist Church of San Sonora, New Mexico. And as near as Eddy could tell, he and Rosilee had shaken hands with about near all of them before spotting a place to sit down. He spotted Uncle Jake and headed for him.

Jake Wilson had sat in that same pew ever since the auditorium had been built. But occasionally a stranger would come in and plop down in his space. None of the regular congregation would dare do so. It was nothing he bragged of, but most people were aware of his generous tithes. When he saw Eddy, he jumped up and started pumping his hand. Rosilee got an even better pumping. Eddy realized the old man wasn't dead yet. He figured the nurses that visited him each week at the hotel surely got their money's worth.

Jake turned and motioned for the others to make room. It was a tight fit and when he finally sat down, Jake enjoyed being close to Rosilee.

Soon the singing started and Rosilee cut loose. He was a little embarrassed but joined in.

Eddy listened intently to the sermon. Then it was time, a time to surrender. Nearly time for him to get his butt out of that pew and walk down that aisle. The page number and title of the invitational hymn was announced and the congregation rose. Eddy sure didn't need a songbook for that one. It was his grandpappy's favorite.

The organist stopped playing as Eddy made his way down the aisle. Rosilee was at his side. The young and proud pastor embraced them.

Not even a baby was whimpering, and with the exception of a few sobs, the church was deathly quiet until a youngster hollered. "Look at that man Mama. Is that Jesus?"

A lot of people could not resist laughing, and Eddy turned and smiled at the young boy. And then he couldn't believe his eyes. It was Sundance coming toward them, wearing his best pair of worn out jeans, an old sports coat, and his long hair and beard.

The three of them committed and the preacher looked out over the congregation.

"This is not Jesus, but a man Jesus has sent to us."

35

*C*ashion Cosmetics had moved its corporate headquarters from San Francisco to Los Angeles and Eddy, Sundance and Rosilee were on their way out. Since Sundance had finally agreed to go, they had opted to just head out across the desert toward California before he had a change of mind.

They stopped and spent the night in Phoenix, calling Mr. and Mrs. Cashion before they went to bed. Great news for the Cashions.

When they arrived, Rosilee wanted to go straight to the offices.

Their cousin, Cuz, who had been running the company in their absence was not so happy to see them. His ambitions had moved him up the corporate ladder and he suddenly feared their return would be a stumbling block for him. And that dark skinned cowboy they had with them would probably be looking for a big piece of the company pie since he was driving Rosilee's car. He probably doesn't own anything but a piece of junk, Cuz thought to himself. And then there was the Prodigal Son.

Cuz shook Eddy's hand and thanked him for all his help, thinking fast on his feet to get on top of the situation. "And Mister Gavolin, what kind of a position would you be looking for with the company?"

Rosilee and Eddy sensed what Cuz was up to. They smiled at each other and Eddy turned and tried to ask with a straight face, "Might you be offering me a job, sir?"

"I just thought you might be interested," Cuz replied, hoping to get to the bottom of this man's intentions.

Eddy slowly looked around the huge office. "It sure would be nice to work in a fancy place like this, but I just can't do it." He paused, and then lied. "I got me about a thousand head to vaccinate and castrate back in New Mexico next week. I could sure use a good man like you to go back and help me if you might be interested in some fresh air and man-work."

Rosilee looked over at her father and laughed. "I don't think you could do without him could you, Mister C?"

The cousin got the point, and with a red face excused himself.

Gloria Drake had slipped quietly back into San Sonora to give birth to Eddy's child, an eight pound, dark skinned, healthy baby boy. She called Checan later in the day and told her the news.

In an hour Checan burst through the door, her face beaming. She rushed to the bed. "What a beautiful baby, Gloria. I just hope Eddy doesn't have a heart attack when he finds out he's the daddy of a bouncing baby boy.

"You said Eddy's in California."

"He headed out there on Monday."

"Think you could get him on the phone for me?"

"We'll sure give it a try," she replied, fishing the number Eddy had given her out of her purse.

"One moment please."

She handed the phone to Gloria.

"Checan, what's up?"

"It's Gloria, Eddy."

He was almost speechless. "Where are you?"

"I'm in San Sonora. What are you doing in California? Courting a movie star?"

"Naw, just brought a couple of friends out here," he replied, feeling a little uneasy.

"Male or female?"

"One of each."

"Would you marry me, Eddy?"

His head felt light as he replied, "Would tonight be too soon?"

"But you're in California."

"Not a problem."

"Eddy, I love you. I would like to spend the rest of my life taking care of you and your son."

"Sounds good to me, but what if our first is a little girl?"

"I'm sitting up in the hospital bed and our first is a little boy, Eddy."

Eddy leaned against Mr. Cashion's desk to keep from falling. "I'll be there as soon as I can. I love you," he said as soon as he got his breath.

When he hung up he turned to Rosilee. "Gloria has given me a son and we're getting married. Can you get me to the airport?"

She laughed as she turned to her father. "How long would it take to get the company plane ready to go, Pop?"

LAUS DEO